My Happy Retreat

A Novel

Toni M. Forsyth

minna
PRESS

Copyright 2014, Toni M. Forsyth.

ISBN 978-976-95693-3-1

Ordering Information
Quantity (Bulk) Sales: Special discounts are available on quantity (bulk) purchases by corporations, associations, and others. For details, contact the publisher:
sales@minnapress.com

Executive Editor: Lena J. Rose

Designer: Mark Steven Weinberger

Published in Kingston, Jamaica
by Minna Press
204 Mountain View Avenue, Kingston 6

Dedication

I dedicate this novel with all of my love to my mother, Ruth Felicia Shepherd Forsyth, who had her own novel published at age 95, and who taught me how to be my own woman, my own person and to believe in myself no matter what.

Table of Contents

Lovers and madmen have such seething brains,
Such shaping fantasies, that apprehend
More than cool reason ever comprehends.
The lunatic, the lover, and the poet
Are of imagination all compact.
One sees more devils than vast hell can hold—
That is the madman. The lover, all as frantic,
Sees Helen's beauty in a brow of Egypt.
The poet's eye, in fine frenzy rolling,
Doth glance from heaven to Earth, from Earth to heaven.
And as imagination bodies forth
The forms of things unknown, the poet's pen
Turns them to shapes and gives to airy nothing
A local habitation and a name.
Such tricks hath strong imagination,
That if it would but apprehend some joy,
It comprehends some bringer of that joy.
Or in the night, imagining some fear,
How easy is a bush supposed a bear!

—A MIDSUMMER'S NIGHT DREAM

Foreword

Jabez was more honorable than his brothers; and his mother called his name Jabez, saying, "Because I bore him in pain." Jabez called upon the God of Israel, saying, "Oh that you would bless me and enlarge my border, and that your hand might be with me, and that you would keep me from harm so that it might not bring me pain!" And God granted what he asked.

1 CHRONICLES 4:9–10

As Director of Psychiatric Services at University Hospital, Paradise Island, The Bahamas, I can confirm that the treatment of geriatric depression as a mental disorder has been in need of urgent attention but is now getting the recognition that it deserves. Because of the large number of returnees to the island who are members of the Baby Boomer generation and are starting to show signs of it—apart from whatever other forms of depression or mental illness may have manifested themselves in their younger days—what was once dismissed as "that's just what happens when you get old" has now become the next personal demon to slay as they are reminded more and more of the likelihood of the decline of their own mental faculties in the years to come.

As we age, "that's just what happens" in terms of the fading minds and memories of our grandparents has morphed into, "I'm already too stressed as it is. I just can't deal with mother or daddy any more." When a Boomer's attempt to let her own aging parents remain in their home fails and they are first moved in with the middle aged Boomer's family to great domestic disruption and ultimate dismay, the decision may finally be made to place mom and dad in an assisted living or even a secure facility. But the problems associated with one's mentally challenged parents no longer being able to care for themselves have now become a swirling chimera of things to come eliciting a level of anxiety and panic in response to a threat hitherto unthinkable. That threat has raised the ontological alarm.

I've come to realize that we all orchestrate our own little realities and delusions as we make the choices that serve to define our lives. But the steady descent into a solitary world of one's own develops over an extended period of time sometimes as a "repackaging" of independently verifiable events. It is a wholly internal process. Typically, for observers both within and outside the immediate family of someone experiencing depressive paranoia or dementia, recognition that something "isn't quite right" or daddy's verbal responses "don't quite make sense anymore" or mother's actions "don't quite fit" the situation may be even slower in becoming apparent. Or, quite the contrary, one could have a situation where a friend, much like the child in the well-known children's story, all of a sudden sees a once appropriately clad but now naked figure and blurts out the obvious truth that "the Emperor has no clothes!" All the townspeople had been going along with the fiction that the emperor was still opulently dressed. They, along with the Emperor, had been seeing only that which they wanted to see, had been conditioned to see, not what the innocent eyes of the child was now witnessing.

For a member of the Boomer generation, of whom the principal narrator of this story is one, the child who speaks truth to power may actually be a son or daughter, a middle aged person themselves now in their late forties or fifties. They have their own kids to raise and educate and shepherd through life's passages, and now their late sixty or seventy-something year-old parents are just beginning to face their own mortality and struggles with the vagaries of the mind. The time is nigh. Mother or daddy has finally lost it, and now it's as clear as day. So that's what was going on all along!

Some of us born during the approximately 20 year period after WWII who were educated abroad, practiced our professions both overseas and here on the island, did well financially and were even able to take early retirement in order to enjoy the fruits of our college-degree-enhanced, success-driven labours. Others of us will need to work for a few more years because the economy or time and chance or all three will not have been as kind. Whatever our financial circumstances, and despite the desperate consumption of organic foods, the lifestyle lifts, the customized exercise routines, the personal trainers, "time and chance happeneth to us all." We will grow old, our bodies will change before our very eyes, we will all eventually look in the mirror one day and say, "Who the hell is that?"

And for some of us, that lack of recognition will become more profound than for others. Alzheimer's or some other form of dementia will silently creep into those "little gray cells" of which Poirot was so proud and transport them into a world of their own making. A world where they forget not only the names of those nearest and dearest to them but their basic connection to them, our basic connection to them. It will be the loss of ties to the present as well as a reconnection to memories and events and people long gone.

My Happy Retreat: A Novel is the story of Me, a woman recently retired and in her early sixties, caught up as the third person in the lives of a well-educated, well-traveled, semi-retired couple, owners of a sugar cane plantation on a Caribbean island, and how she came to be swept up in—or allowed herself to be swept up in depending on your views about locus of control—the gradual slipping away of the wife's grip on reality. The chronological ages of the narrator and the couple with whom she became involved span only a decade, but their mental states during the course of their association grew to be light years apart. The cold revelation here is that any one of us who reaches this stage of our lives at any time may start losing touch with the world of forms and end up responding to the world of ideas that exist inside our heads. When that happens, the problem will no longer be a case of merely forgetting where we placed the keys to the car, but of losing the ability to articulate or to even comprehend what exactly is the purpose for which the car is used.

Geriatric depression, paranoia, anxiety and panic are all treatable conditions, but when they are precursors to Alzheimer's or dementia, the prognosis for now is that there is no cure. Medication and Mindfulness

Therapy may be useful tools for mitigating their effects, but the condition must be properly diagnosed by first ruling out any physiological causes for changes in behavior or physical symptoms such as elevated blood pressure and heart rate. These could signal physiological malfunctions or the onset of a mental meltdown—a panic or anxiety attack—or changes in eating or activity levels may occur that could indicate the onset of major clinical depression. What becomes necessary next are first hand accounts of observed behavior by those who actually live with the person who seems to be wandering off into realms experienced only by the identified person herself.

My Happy Retreat is a glimpse into a world of self-delusion. As a psychiatrist, I have had decades of witnessing the effects of clinical depression, anxiety and paranoia first hand. I hope that in taking the journey with the author and her protagonist back in time through the account of events that delineate the shape and texture, colour and hue of the principal characters and their lives, the reader will come to appreciate the symmetry of forms, the play of light and shadow that illuminate who we are not only now, but perhaps who we may become in the future.

Bridget Peterson, M.D.
Director of Psychiatric Services, University Hospital
Paradise Island, The Bahamas
September 15, 2014

Prologue

Do not go gentle into that good night...
Rage, rage against the dying of the light.
— DYLAN THOMAS

A prologue is meant to be a sign post for those who have the desire for some kind of thesis, some kind of main point, some morsel of clarification served up to act as a first course in anticipation of what is to come. It is a statement for the purpose of "making sense," as in "On what basis will I be able to make sense of this that awaits me?" It precedes the discrete bits and pieces of the grand narrative that follows. It is that which has been deduced (in this case) by an omniscient eye based on a compilation of facts and plausible fictions where the facts are unknown or must be disguised, events and happenings that have revealed themselves or been revealed over an extended period of time. Indeed, a lifetime.

I think a writer certainly has the prerogative to declare (or not to declare) his or her intent in advance of that which is to follow. In fact, there are some who would say that an author actually has a responsibility to declare, because the slow process of induction may not necessarily serve the storyteller so very well in the early stages of the storytelling, that is, in the short run. The reader may only be willing to commit a limited amount of time to making up his or her mind as to whether to proceed with the text immediately in front, to quickly move on to that which follows or to unceremoniously absent himself or herself from the work entirely, once and for all. In actual fact, however, the storyteller must rely on both the deductive and the inductive, both analysis and commentary as she weaves her tale because even though providing some initial sense of direction may be satisfying to some, it is both the art and skill of revelation that holds the reader through to the very end. Any artifice that helps to serve that end— such as an elaborate prologue—should be employed. Can be employed. It's okay to use it. And artifice it is indeed because there is a conscious mind at work deciding when and where to use whatever device may be at her disposal. The trick is to use it well.

This book is a fictional narrative based on the events chronicled in the journals of one of Dr. Bridget Peterson's patients. It describes the post retirement life of a female protagonist simply referred to as "Me." As presented here, and incorporated along with the ongoing commentaries and analyses of "The Author," some of what the reader will see is taken directly from the journal entries of "Me" and some from her e-mail correspondences to friends and to the well known newspaper advice columnist, "Abigail." The reader must therefore understand that the "I" throughout the novel is a shifting persona, a changing point-of-view.

The whole "Happy Retreat" meme as used here seems to have taken on more of a life of its own than what I had originally imagined: it isn't just about the protagonist's happy retreat into her Baby Boomer retirement years or even the plantation owners' happy retreat into the life of the landed gentry, or even about the past or future happy retreats of others. My Happy Retreat (both upper and lower case) is about control—who has it, who doesn't, how one gets it, how one maintains it and how one manages to try and wrest some of it away from the tight fisted grip of others in order to hold onto it for oneself despite the best efforts of those who would like to not let that happen. It's about how we observe it in action as children growing up and how we can mistake what we think to be the real thing (that is, real control) isn't really.

It is also about what is verifiably real and what isn't, what is fantasy or illusion, what others observe to be actually happening versus what only one's self can see as filtered through the unique lens of one's own personal point-of-view.

We make choices as children about our lives and how we will ultimately live them as adults at incredibly young ages—2, 3, 5, 6, 8, 12, 18, 21—based on what we think we see happening, what we think is going on when what we think we see is really not what is happening at all. And sometimes we stick with those choices for the rest of our lives when, if we had only been able to dig a little deeper, see a little bit more clearly–with a more mature eye, through a glass a little less darkly tinted–we might have been able to discern a different path and actually have chosen a different approach to being-in-the-world.

The child who sees his mother tell an older sibling to return the toy that the older one snatched from the younger may see women as wielding great power. Or that same mother at another time, rushing to offer assistance or make sure that the house is less noisy, less chaotic when an ailing grandparent comes to live may seem to be herself beholding to a more quiet, unspoken kind of authority. Or perhaps to a more belligerent and bellicose authority. Who is in control of whom and when and to what extent? And when a teenage son raises his voice to a father who is intent on bullying his mother just one time too many? And when the father actually backs down? And when the mother finally speaks up? Who really is wielding control then? At what point do we each take control—either consciously or unconsciously—of how we are going to live our lives?

At what point do we either consciously or unconsciously choose for ourselves the values against which we will measure the decisions that define us as who we are as unique human beings? And at what point do some of us either consciously or unconsciously decide to disengage from the reality of the actual people and events playing out before us and choose to allow our fantasies to author the script that is played out on the stage where we enact our parts and attempt to make others play out theirs as written far, far in advance of the performance that eventually reaches the theater at hand?

"The Author"

Mr.

For now, tellingly enough, "Mr." gets to be defined by means and in terms of his relationship to the women in his life.

Fifty plus years ago a twenty-one year-old aspiring actress in a national little theater production company who had a great body and a pretty face made a conscious decision to lure an eighteen year-old high school boy away from his eighteen year old, drop dead gorgeous high school girlfriend. For some time the young actress had seen the boy around town at numerous parties and get-togethers where other girls had unabashedly fluttered and fallen all over him because of his good looks, athleticism and genuinely good-hearted personality. Maybe it went to his head, but he was also very smart—top of the class smart—but that part really wasn't heading the list of attributes for which most of the girls were pursuing him.

Over the summer that followed the last of his final exams, the eighteen year-old girlfriend took a three-week trip with her mother to visit relatives in Cuba. The mother invited the boy to come along. His mother said no. Clearly a little bit much too much for her baby boy. A trip like that would have smacked of some kind of public–if not actual familial–declaration of something an eighteen year old boy with a very bright future should not be declaring.

The young *actrice* took the opportunity during the girlfriend's absence to flirt with the boy–now really a young man–at parties as only a woman who is totally comfortable with her body can and socialized more freely with him at various events around town. The mother-who-was-visiting-relatives-in-Cuba along with her daughter heard about the territorial incursion from vigilant friends back home again tried to get the boy's mother to let the son come visit if only for a week. She again refused thinking that she didn't want "that kind of pressure" placed on her boy. He was much too young, had his whole life ahead of him and the whole world was impatiently awaiting his arrival to be so demonstrably tied to any one girl no matter how beautiful she was or how good the family from which she came. The mother and daughter came back from their vacation clearly the worse for the emotional wear.

After that summer, the boy's relationship with his high school sweetheart was never the same. He once again began to openly date other girls including the aspiring actress.

Just before New Year's Eve rolled around, the *ingenue* found herself in the enviable position of having two suitors vying for the pleasure of her company at the various parties that were to be held around town. One was a long time boyfriend, a regular amongst those in her somewhat sophisticated group of theatre types and their associates. The other invitation was from the former high school boy, now become a young man, working as an accountant in order to save enough money to go off to college in a couple of years.

With whom should the actress go? Known about town as a PYT (Pretty Young Thing), she told herself that she would see just how much power she actually held in sway over the two suitors and just how earnest the still eighteen year old former high school student was by orchestrating a little test—a challenge as it were. Having told the other fellow that he was to pick her up at 7 pm, she then told our hapless young man that he was to pick her up at 7:10 pm sharp. The rest is history. The first fellow was a few minutes late—16 minutes to be exact—as was often his wont, and our young man was actually a little early—as was his custom. And the rest is history.

Upon this caprice the die was cast for more than the next half century of the young man's life. Such is the nature of fate and of such are the vagaries that serve to define our existence in this world.

And of such stuff are made the stories that we tell ourselves in order to endure.

*H*er story begins with her mother, a young civil servant in a rural town on the eastern end of the island near the end of the third decade of the 20th century. The town was a shipping port from whence bananas and sugar were sent on their way to markets in the U.K. The agricultural crops were grown and harvested across the vast expanses of lands acquired after the English routed the Spanish from their early conquests throughout most of the Caribbean. She was the product of several centuries of miscegenation–the sexual coupling of the white and black races, the European and the African. There had been no indigenous peoples found at that end of the island during the early conquests so the bloodlines were clearly established. The mother was an attractive young woman, and Mrs. was the product of her mother's affair with an English civil engineer. He had left his young family behind in England for an extended period of time—but less than a year—to work on establishing a more efficient mechanical system for the production of refined sugar from the harvested cane.

The mother wanted more than anything to escape the claustrophobia of life in the tiny village where she had grown up with no opportunities available other than to marry some underpaid manager in a dry goods store or accountant, or teacher or minor public official. Any such union would still result in a life to be lived primarily within the few square miles of the town in which she was born. She didn't want to be trapped there forever. Upon leaving secondary school, she had gotten a job in the local post office distributing the mail brought in either by boat or by horse drawn conveyance. There were very few automobiles being used at the time in these small enclaves of island life, and the arrival of the young white man who had one of the few automobiles around for miles posed possibilities that she could only have dreamed of before.

He checked-in for his mail every day. He began to flirt with her and eventually she with him. The chance for a real courtship at first were essentially non-existent because everybody knew the majority of these young white men from England were deployed to temporary posts in the colonies for such a short time. Nevertheless, her parents invited him over and he began to come to tea at her home on Saturday and Sunday afternoons. He then asked permission for her to accompany him on a drive in his automobile through the countryside, a Ford made in America, on those Sunday afternoons. Her parents thought that just maybe, just maybe he might decide to remain on the island if he were to fall in love with their daughter. Not totally unheard of. Even though he was married. These things had been known to happen, and they loved their daughter and wanted her to be happy and after all, he was such a nice young man, and showed no signs of prejudice whatsoever (but she was fair-skinned anyway—what qualifies in island parlance as a "browning"—so...).

In the end, because of those Sunday drives in the American built automobile, she got pregnant. He of course had no intention of abandoning his wife and child back home in England. The young woman eventually went to Capital City on the other side of the island before she started to really show. She had the child at the home of relatives who had been told that her husband had been called back to England but would eventually send for her.

The mother studied for and took the civil service exam and applied for a supervisory position at the Parish Council Office back home in her small town. She took her baby daughter back with her and decided that she would raise her with an iron glove. The young civil servant, now an embittered woman, would tell the child along with everyone else that her husband had died six months after the child was born and before he could send for them to join him in England. It was a lie of course, but it also provided plausible deniability. The daughter of course eventually found out the truth.

In the mind of the mother, the child's racially enhanced bloodline now dictated that she was really too good to associate with the mostly darker skinned children around where she lived. So the girl spent all of her time that wasn't in the company of her mother or grandparents or later at school in the house with the housemaid, amusing herself, fantasizing about what it would be like to be free to play and dance and sing with other children and have fun. She danced by herself, sang to herself, made up little plays in her head in which she was always the lead and acted out the other parts as well. Her fantasy life was rich, but she still longed to be in the company of other children her age whom she could see outside of her window happily cavorting in the sun.

And then the day came with the news that changed her life forever.

She was to go to a boarding school several hours journey away from her home and her pathologically controlling mother, and away from the house where her doting grandparents lived. The school had a name with the word "happy" in it so she knew it would be a wonderful place to be. And best of all she would be free to be with other children, to associate with other little people like herself with no one to dictate whether or not they met the impossible standards of class and color and status set by her mother.

 And she thrived. She was smart, she was good at sports, she was good at everything to which she put her mind, and her most natural inclination was to put her mind more toward athletics than academics whenever she could get away with it. Which obviously wasn't for overly extended periods of time because her mother kept tabs on her even from a distance, consulting with the headmaster of the school about her academic progress at every step of the way. But above all she was happy! And by the time she graduated from high school and went back to Capital City on the other side of the island to find work, she was ready to avail herself of all the excitement it had to offer. And eventually she found herself joining a newly formed theater and dance performance group and she was in heaven!

The country girl became the sophisticated city girl working in a bank by day and training with the theater company in the afternoons and evenings and on weekends. And then she got to perform before a live audience and she knew her life had truly begun. She was talented, she was pretty and she had a terrific body. She had all kinds of admirers and she enjoyed the attention and the company of her new friends. Her social life was off the charts. She could pick, choose and refuse from among the many young men who saw the talented young woman perform on stage. Her life was glamorous, she had her own income, and her mother's controlling reach had long been banished to the outskirts of her existence.

Her aspirations now knew no bounds and soon she began to dream of expanding her horizons even further, of testing the waters in other lands. Perhaps Paris, perhaps New York. Really, were there any limits now? Hadn't the door been fully opened, the curtain lifted revealing an immense arena where she could be free to be and to live her life with the whole world as her stage, with all the people in it her audience and bask in their admiration and explore it all just as she pleased? And to shop and to buy pretty clothes and pretty shoes and all the sparkly and exciting things she could only dream about as a child closed up tight in her mother's house, squashed like a trapped lightening bug under her mother's thumb?

And then one night she arrived at one of the many parties that were taking place around town on the weekends and saw a really good looking boy, maybe 18 or so, drive up in a red sports car. He had a ton of girls flocking around him by the time he got inside including one really beautiful girl who was apparently his date for the evening. The actress had guys hanging around her as well, but she already knew them all and was bored with every one of them. But this kid looked interesting. She even thought of him as a kid because she could tell he was younger than she was—probably by a few years, maybe as much as five. Didn't matter. He had caught her eye. She would make it a point to find out more about him. But don't show too much interest that night, she told herself. Not the first time around. Just keep her eyes and options open and see what happens down the road.

He had graduated with distinctions in all of his Cambridge Advanced Examination subjects by the beginning of that summer. In order to save money to go to university in England to study engineering he needed a job. He found one. Where? In the bank where the actress worked! She had continued to see him and his red car and his girlfriend at parties all over town but she could see he was what was known as a "girly man." The girls liked him, he liked the girls. Obviously too conceited to be worth the trouble, but now here he was practically on her doorstep. They conversed, but she wasn't going to let him think she was his for the taking. Besides, he really was just a boy right out of high school and being a part of theater life had conferred on her a level of sophistication and savvy that made him, at least at that point worthy only of marginal interest. But she thought he was really good looking, and she really liked and really wanted good-looking, shiny new things. And there was that red sports car.

The rest, as they say, is history.

Me

Dear Abigail:

At what seems to me to be a rather late stage in life and as an aging Baby Boomer, I find myself in an increasingly untenable situation. I have either lost, misplaced, or while I wasn't paying attention someone stole my locus of control, my sense of personal agency over said life. I seem to have become enamoured of and because of a recent illness physically dependent upon an attractive, caring and incredibly nurturing man who is 8 years older than I and who is the owner of a sizable plantation estate. I am currently a tenant on that estate enjoying the delights of living in a tiny, impossibly cramped one bedroom apartment located just a hundred yards or so away from the large, impressive great house. Several years ago I rented the place for what I thought would be a short term—six months, a year or so at the most—while my own house was being built about two miles away. But now I find myself writing to you, desperately in need of your help in order to regain some sense of independence and control, which I have totally lost, over my life.

—*Confused*

Advice columnist Abigail von Nostrum welcomes all inquiries sent to her at this newspaper but regrets that she cannot provide personal responses to individual letter writers.

After a successful but very stressful career as an academic, I took early retirement, moved to a tropical paradise and looked forward to living in the house of my dreams—tailor made to my specifications—traveling, entertaining and engaging in intellectual pursuits wherever they might take me. However, after over five years of construction woes and after having spent a small fortune on the entire endeavour, my house is still not finished and remains entangled by cost overruns, its construction beleaguered by incompetent workmanship and

TONI M. FORSYTH

plagued by the prospect of many more months of remedial work before I can move into even a half completed house. Literally, half of the house will still be without a roof when I move in.

In addition, the stress and anxiety caused by a culturally based economic pathology that apparently forms the basis for most of the contractual undertakings here, the stupefying ineptitude and the lack of ethical business practices (according to 1st world norms) on the part of local building contractors (I'm on my fifth and counting) along with the repercussions from trying to be a socially responsible member of my new community and a good Samaritan to boot (by providing substantial financial assistance to several locals who were in financial need) have resulted in my developing a serious, potentially fatal heart condition.

By now one might well surmise that the "increasingly untenable situation" to which I alluded at the beginning of this letter has to do with my home construction project from hell or with my out-of-the-blue medical problem. But what prompts this particular missive, however, has to do with the very first revelation mentioned: that of being untenably dependent upon an immensely personable, kind and incredibly nurturing man. But, "Wonderful!" you say. And at your age too! *Mazel tov!* you say. But hold on, before you get too carried away to

> *...some melodious plot*
> *Of beechen green, and shadows numberless*

—wait, wait for it—he's married!   Abigail, I can hear your own (and your readers' collective) "Oh, my God!" and even as I write, I visualize the accompanying rolling of eyes and hear the weeping and wailing and gnashing of teeth, but please hear me out, masochist that I seemingly am. For so many reasons I am desperately out of control of my life and don't know how to regain it. Or, conversely, I do know how but am turning myself inside out trying to find an alternative solution to the obvious.

My heart aches, and a drowsy numbness pains
My sense, as though of hemlock I had drunk,
Or emptied some dull opiate to the drains
One minute past, and Lethe-wards had sunk.

The very first thing I need to say is that neither the man nor his wife were happy campers in terms of their marriage way before the time that I first came along. We're talking over 50 years of not being happy campers. They both told me so in private conversations independently of each other. Mr. showed it and acted it out from time to time taking his ill-tempered frustrations out on her. She, not quite so subtly, showed her displeasure and long suffering to anyone who cared to see. They both fleshed out their narratives to me over the ensuing months.

'Tis not through envy of thy happy lot,
But rather being too happy in thine happiness,
That thou, light-wingéd dryad of the trees
In some melodious plot of beechen green
And shadows numberless
Singest of summer in full-throated ease.

The strong feelings of care and concern for, perhaps even infatuation or hero worship (as in "my hero") that have developed with regards to Mr. and the dependency upon him that I am now experiencing are based on some serious rescue activity on his part that took almost four years of relationship building before they could even have begun to take place. It wasn't until almost the end of year four of our association as tenant and landlord that they emerged. Over the course of that time span, I had been slowly, systematically drawn into the domestic drama that was his marriage. Because of the generational more so than the absolute age difference between myself and my landlords, one could say that the drama in the making between us actually started when I was about ten years old— or perhaps even before I was born.

I was initially drawn into their world of quiet marital desperation shortly after I first rented the apartment located on the plantation. Right from the very beginning my landlords—Mr. and Mrs.—offered me a standing invitation to tea at the Great House between 4:30 and 5:00 pm every day. I was informed that it was a daily routine and that I should just pop over whenever I wanted. I didn't really follow through with any regularity on what seemed to be a somewhat intrusive undertaking. Occasionally, I would call and inquire whether my landlords, whom I eventually began to regard as friends, were going to be having tea at the appointed hour and would receive an assurance in the affirmative and be asked if I would like to join them which I almost always did. But eventually, I tended more and more to wait for specific invitations rather than take what began to seem to me to be the liberty of simply presenting myself at the door at the designated hour or of even taking the initiative to call in advance.

During those afternoon teas, the topics of many stimulating discussions ranged from the state of island politics and scandals to issues involving other countries and U.S. policies at home and abroad. There were also forays into subjects of a more philosophical nature. Both my landlord and myself are passionate, highly opinionated debaters. We exist, in fact, on opposite sides of the political spectrum—he being staunchly conservative and me being staunchly liberal. The intellectual passion we exhibited was indeed at times inordinately intense with occasions when Mrs. would kick him under the table to indicate that he had crossed some sort of line as host and with me left wondering if in a fit of apoplexy I was going to burst a blood vessel or have a stroke on the spot in response to what I considered to be some of his more egregious right-of-center points of view.

For me, the energy behind my own intense perspectives came from having grown up in a family that thrived on debate and from having an older brother (13 years difference) who argued long and hard with complete dispassion about why my views of the world were not only irrational but intellectually inferior to his, thus systematically inculcating me with the belief that others as well would no doubt experience me as being intellectually inferior. And even though as the years passed and I achieved a doctorate degree from a major research university and became an academic in my own right, I continued to hold two simultaneous yet opposing views of myself—one as a respected professor who was comfortable with and who constantly honed her intellectual skills and the other as an intellectual subordinate who over and over again was always in the position of having to prove herself worthy of the right to even sit at the table of debate.

Not too long into the routine of these afternoon teas, I began to realize that I was repeatedly re-enacting a childhood drama/trauma with Mr. In fact, this was not "some" childhood drama, for me it was THE childhood drama. The grand narrative of my life. The script had been written years before, directed and enacted over the course of myriad previous performances with my brother, the dialogue of which had informed my subsequent interactions with every male throughout my entire life. Amazing what an impact one sibling can have on another.

I was a late-in-life child—one that came along after the initial family was essentially grown. My eldest sister was 18 years older than I, my second sister 17 years older and my brother 13 years older. I was not expected. By the time I came along, my father was just embarking on the final incarnation of his professional career and was almost constantly at work trying to earn enough money so that he and my mother could retire early and comfortably on the island paradise of my father's birth. He succeeded. He was physically around while I was growing up, but in a sense not really present (he was always at work during the days and sometimes slept at his place of business because of hellish hours and a fear of burglaries) until I was about 13 years old. By then he was retired and, for the most part, an elderly man with whom I had almost nothing in common.

My relationship with my brother filled the vacuum left by my father's virtual absence. That relationship was my model for all of my subsequent interactions with men. Not particularly supportive, not nurturing, at times tyrannical, perhaps even mildly (whatever that means) abusive. The

TONI M. FORSYTH

constant playful threat from my brother was always, "I'm going to beat you up." or "I'm going to tickle you to death." while chasing me around the house with much laughter and glee. There was also one memorable episode where he sucked up my waist length hair up into the vacuum cleaner. An undertaking which he thought was great fun but which was actually quite frightening to me. It is only recently that I have come to recognize what my brother was to me then and to a large extent who he still is now as compared to who I had managed to fool myself into believing he was throughout the course of our lives. Not that he doesn't love me or that I don't love him, but it's a complicated kind of love as so many family relationships are.

My mother, God rest her soul, created and managed the on-going fiction that he was my protector, and it is only now that the puppet mistress in our family is gone that the illusion has disintegrated and the reality behind the performance has seen the light of day. He was not my emotional or psychological protector. (Nor perhaps should he have been expected to be.) We are very different personalities. Because he is who he is and I was who I am, the effect he had on me was to routinely undermine any stabilizing sense of self in relation to men that I might have been able to develop while growing up. He undermined my sense of self worth as a female and as an intelligent, lovable human being. Not deliberately in principle or with malicious intent but systematically in the day-to-day living of my childhood life. Not *de jure* but *de facto*. It's just the way it worked out.

All three of my siblings had an entirely different experience with my parents and of family life than I did. They grew up with a fully engaged father. With me, my brother, by default was my father figure growing up and as such helped me to shape an image of myself that has always been filled with self-doubt not only in terms of my intellectual capabilities but also in terms of my inherent sense of self worth both as a person and as a female. I don't think he particularly likes women. I don't know why, I can't guess. His wife is/was more or less a tomboy. He passed on an early girlfriend who was intellectually, professionally and socially his equal and who was a real looker (as they say) for the less academically ambitious and not particularly socially mobile tomboy. Go figure. That's another story, but perhaps that bit of information helps to add another dab of paint to the mural of how I got from "there" to "here" and finally to "over yonder"—wherever that is—and where, of course, I ultimately want to be: more in control.

So now, back to several years of afternoon teas averaging about three to four times per week. I got to know Mrs. better in between the times when Mr. had to retreat from our heated debates (or had not yet appeared) to attend to something property related. She and I would also talk during the few times we spent together in the car going into town to run errands. The errand-running time together was relatively short lived in terms of occurrences because Mrs. is an inveterate shopper and I am not. I absolutely loathe the pursuit of the pastime called "shopping." I also cannot abide "chatter." I'll debate and discuss, but constant, mindless chatter drives me nuts. I also hate being the driver on long distance trips and freak out at the prospect of getting lost which I so easily seem to do. The couple of times that Mrs. and I made the long drive into Capital City utilizing her navigating skills, we got lost—once, big time. We never drove in together without Mr. again.

Over the course of years two and three of our developing friendship, I learned from Mrs. what she considered to be the true nature of her relationship with Mr. I had no idea at the time that her revelations to me were, in fact, not just the spontaneous fruit of intimate "girl-talk" but rather had within them what I now believe to be the seeds of a self-serving but ultimately fatal (to me) agenda. Awareness alert! I do not mean to portray myself as the victim of a nefarious plot. It's just that I now believe that because I had been deemed "safe" (more about what that means later), I was deliberately being given the "go ahead" signal for what was intended to be a "special" friendship with Mr., sanctioned by Mrs. and complete with explanations of why such largesse on her part was beneficial for all concerned.

What I learned was this: Mr. is, as I described earlier, what is called in these parts a "girly" man. Having previously only heard that phrase come from the lips of a California governor with regard to what he believed to be a description of the members of the state legislature, I told her that I did not know what it meant. She said that it referred to men who really appreciated women—who enjoyed the company of women. Okay.

She went on to say that she knew what he was like when she married him but that she let him know that it was alright for him to have women as friends but that he just couldn't sleep with them. Okay.

She named two women that I knew who were already serving in this capacity albeit because of time and distance constraints on a limited basis. No sex, just friends who occasionally communicated with him and spent a couple of hours enjoying his company in person two or three times a year. One was most likely a lesbian (according to him), the other perhaps twelve or more years older than he.

Once there had been a very sexy young Cuban woman who had briefly lived in one of the rental units on the property several years before who had been pointedly designated as off-limits by Mrs. for any kind of relationship. But I was deemed to be acceptable. Even though I was neither a lesbian nor significantly older, I was considered by Mrs. to be "not his type," so I was no threat. Safe. Go figure.

But I also learned something about Mr. from Mr. himself during one of our one-on-one drives into the city. It was something that Mrs. had never said a word about to me. When he was younger and relatively early in his marriage, while he was on an extended business trip in Scandinavia, he had had a months long intense affair with a girl who opened up a new world of sexual freedom to him. There were hot tubs and open nudity and a relaxed attitude toward the human body that he had never experienced before. The girl fell hard for him and he for her. When it was time for him to return to London and to his wife and two young children, she wanted to come with him. She couldn't understand why not. She wanted to call and speak to Mrs. directly to see if they couldn't work out some kind of man-sharing arrangement involving the three of them and the two kids. Mrs. was not interested. Not even interested in discussing any of the various possibilities for alternative living arrangements that were being presented. She eventually opted to give him another chance at marital fidelity and monogamy. She maintained the locus of control over the situation. With few protests he eventually acquiesced. Life went on. History would repeat itself two more times.

Forty-four years later, neither of them had managed to find genuine happiness in their marital relationship. Mrs. did not want to be living on a rural farm on an island nation with a man who could be bitingly sarcastic and controls all aspects of their finances, decisions about the house, its furnishings, the gardens, their social engagements, what and when they should eat, etc.—and would rather be living near London, closer proximity to one of their children, with transportation, social and cultural outlets waiting just outside her front door.

When does she get her turn? Where is her locus of control? Where has the young performer gone who had a sense of personal agency as opposed to the traditional housewife who now continues to allow herself to be acted upon, on behalf of? Where is the person who propelled herself to embark on a precarious path to freedom (by getting pregnant out of wedlock) in order to escape her mother's oppression and the confines of life on a small island—a path that was fraught with moral censure and social condemnation? I do not believe that any half way intelligent woman "accidentally" gets pregnant. There's a whole lot of conscious activity that transpires before the deed is actually done. And she was three years older and more sophisticated than he was (not just "experienced" sexually although she was that too), and he didn't see her even then as the love of his life, and in her heart she probably knew it—him being a "girly man" and all. How does one exercise control?

By any means necessary.

What I have learned about Mr., on the other hand, is that he is at heart a romantic who later in life was in love with an idea, the idea of becoming a gentleman farmer, a proper English squire—but he has now become hard pressed to find the love in the grunge work associated with the maintenance of a large property constantly in need of attention (the nature of the beast), or in the reality of crops lacking sufficient yield, or inadequate markets

TONI M. FORSYTH

incapable of providing the profits that could pay for the upkeep of an entire estate much less earn anything approaching a disposable income. Nor does he love the continuing hassle of dealing with workers who under perform and cause endless problems. As one gets older, juggling while standing on one foot and trying to keep all the balls in the air while chewing gum all at the same time becomes an increasingly difficult task.

Mr. enjoys engaging in stimulating social interactions and animated discourse. He claims that he would love to travel to marvelous locations around the world with an intellectual and spiritual equal, a companion who keeps him stimulated and expands his consciousness along with his sense of self. Mrs., for all of her cooing and soothing ministrations, is not and could never be that person.

For all of his take-charge ability, it would seem that he is doing exceedingly little to create the kind of life that he says he would enjoy and that could make him feel truly alive. Where is his sense of personal agency, his locus of control that would support the life that he claims that he would like for himself in the remaining years of his life? For now, he is casting his nets upon the waters of "busy work." He is mowing lawns and slaying weeds, directing traffic across the vast expanse of the land for which he is responsible. The work is acceptable; it is useful. It keeps him from thinking about how he could actually go about making the people who are closest to him (including himself) happier than they are now.

So I could stop here having outlined the major players in the drama that is currently my life. I know what one solution to my problem of loss of control would be. But there's so much more of the story to tell and retell about the principal players here at My Happy Retreat that I'll stop here for now and come back with more later on.

*M*rs. was not happy to have left their international, cosmopolitan lifestyle to return to the island of their birth to live out the rest of her days on a rural farm. They had been living the glamorous life of British expatriates with Mr. taking on sometimes months long assignments for the British Foreign and Commonwealth Office as well as for the U.N. in Africa, the Middle East and other parts of the world—all of which she had to give up: the life of social niceties, of ladies' charities, the club, of watching Mr. play cricket or squash, of houseboys and cooks and gardeners and yard boys and gate keepers, of endless chatter and dressing up. Life at My Happy Retreat over the course of a twenty-year period had not been what she—perhaps either of them—had hoped it would be. There were indeed teas and hosting dinners for ten or twelve indoors, or sixteen or twenty or thirty in the outdoor pavilion, but somehow it was never quite the same.

The cash flow had almost consistently been negative. A few years before I arrived, she had been working outside the home, but had retired and then sold her car and they were consequently left with only one, barely held together, clattering, 4-wheel drive vehicle primarily used for transporting workers and equipment around the estate for all vehicular travel between them. She missed the autonomy provided by having her own comfortable sedan and also missed being able to drive into the capital city to socialize with friends. A few years back, and from time to time, they would drive in together and spend the night at her mother's house in the city, but she eventually passed away and the house was sold. It now seemed to be such a long drive into town, and Mr. was reluctant to impose on his relatives by staying in one of their homes overnight (although they seemed more than willing to have them as guests) or spending the money on a hotel. So their link to a more sophisticated, more intellectual and even artistic group of friends was lost.

With her daily life now more or less confined within the walls of the house and the boundaries of the estate, Mrs. expressed to me her unhappiness that Mr. was wont to demand his mid-day meal at the exact minute that he arrived from his morning oversight of the farm. She found his attitude towards her and other behavior demanding and unreasonable. From time to time he also made sarcastic remarks directed at Mrs. I do not want to minimize or seem to underestimate what I think was the very real nature and overall experience of being unhappy in her marital situation. It was not the kind of unhappy that comes from outright abuse, but the kind of unhappiness that is the product of deep rooted frustration and the kind of mean spiritedness that can develop as the result of two people who are constantly together living lives of quiet desperation. Both were/are so very dissatisfied with not only their physical but their emotional lives as well—a kind of profound emptiness had settled into both their hearts and had left a hollow space where genuine spirit had once resided.

After so many afternoons of the taking of cups of tea, at this point in my own life at My Happy Retreat I have only just begun to understand the origins, the depth and breadth of the emotional emptiness that I see lying not so far beneath the surface after finally being told the actual history behind how they came to be married in the first place. That understanding does not mitigate the effect that being part of a triangle has had upon me, but the historical background and the contemplation of my position in the vast scheme of things here on the property may help me to better cope and the reader to better understand my place as one of the bit characters (props?) on the stage and better help me to direct my next steps in order to deal with the situation.

I do realize in telling this story that I deliberately keep coming back to the story of the origins of her birth, the pathology of her mother's exercise of control in her early childhood and the circumstances surrounding her marriage to Mr. It's almost as if I am channeling Kierkegaard, imagining the various scenarios under which Abraham sets out on his journey with his son Isaac in order to offer his beloved child as a sacrifice to a capriciously demanding God. The retelling of a tale is a mechanism by which to better understand the thoughts that inform and the emotions that guide our decisions. It is the logic that we employ in order to make the choices that we make, do the things that we do.

I am trying to understand and am trying to help the reader to understand precisely what event or events there may have been, what discrete detail or details in her early development—now open to examination—that eventually allowed her to justify her decision to rise up and dictate the how and when and where of the movements of the person with whom she had previously played the subservient. The permission for her to act according to a certain script, the model for her behavior emanated from her earliest experiences, her earliest emotions. As a child she rightfully craved and needed the companionship of her peers. She longed for the camaraderie, the feeling of joy, the lightness of spirit that playing with other children, that having fun would bring. But someone more powerful was able to deny that kind of happiness to a child. To wield that kind of power meant to be in control of the universe. If Mrs. ever needed to be in control of her universe, it would be those tactics that she would need to employ. God help anyone who thought otherwise. It could mean their demise.

So now we begin, much like Kierkegaard who, in constructing the narrative background to support his seminal philosophy, tells the story of Abraham over and over and over again, taking his reader on multiple versions of a journey that had been scripted from above.

TONI M. FORSYTH

Mistress of the Universe:
Part 2

(To Whom It May Concern: "Mrs." And More About "Mrs." together count as "Mistress of the Universe, Part 1." Carry on.)

Once upon a time, many, many years ago (a lifetime really), when Mr. was eighteen, he was Mr. Hot Catch in the eyes of all the daughters and all the mothers alike within the best social circles of Paradise Island's capital city. He was attractive, athletic and the life of every party he attended. He was also wickedly smart having aced all of his Advanced Level final exams and would be applying for university scholarships after working for a couple of years in banking in order to put some money aside as a cushion for when he was ready to embark on his new life off the island. But one striking young beauty had already caught his attention, and by the time the summer holidays had gotten underway, they had already become an item on the social scene.

Her family had relatives in the Bahamas and her mother decided that she and her daughter would embark on a three-week visit that July. Seeing the potential for an immediate investment, the girl's mother invited Mr. to accompany them perceiving a need to actively insert herself in shaping the future of the youthful romance and believing herself to be the quintessential chaperone. But his mother adamantly refused the invitation for all of the obvious reasons, not the least of which was that she thought her darling boy was far too young and vulnerable to be so conspicuously attached to one young woman. Tongues would wag, assumptions would be made, conclusions would be drawn. And then there were the raging hormones that everyone knew were notoriously clever enough to outsmart even the most diligent eye. No. They would have to wait until the end of July to see each other again. Probably a good idea anyway. Let things cool off a bit. Never a good idea to let things heat up too quickly. Besides. Give the boy a chance not to tie himself down too quickly. Good point. Not at his age. Way too young. Saved by the bell. Next.

Mrs. did not reveal her true self to me. Do we really ever willingly reveal our true selves? Hear me out. She painted a picture, an illusion, a sketch, a landscape if you will of what she wanted me to believe as the truth. (So what else is new you say?) That is what performing artists do—actors, musicians, dancers. With the stroke of a brush, the wave of a hand, the arch of an eyebrow, the riff of a chord, the swish of skirt they make you believe.

Mr. relayed the complete story, filling in the blanks, providing the details, telling the story of her young life with the attention to detail as it was meant to be told. Whereas before there had been actual deception in the recounting of her early life—not just mere illusion—the truth allowed me to finally make sense of what was now becoming a more coherent series of events.

Actual deception? By that I'm addressing her portrayal of the circumstances surrounding her birth. The circumstances surrounding her marriage. The circumstances that have informed her active promotion (supposedly on his behalf) of the cultivation of women as friends but with the explicit caveat of not having sex with them (which dictum, of course, he would sometimes ignore).

Here it is, one more time, because I'm trying to grasp it in different words with different shapes and forms in order to better understand: A careful depiction of Mrs. growing up in a rural town with a mother who considered herself and her daughter better than and socially superior to the other families and children who lived nearby was presented to me over a period of many months of afternoon cups of tea. The father, I was told by Mrs., had died when she was 6 months old. The mother held a minor civil service position in the town. Class differences were a fact of life, still a painful reality here on Paradise Island as indeed is the case in many (most?) third world countries. The economic disparities can be crushing and life altering. It used to be that way in Europe as well. Perhaps not so much anymore, perhaps more so with regard to recent immigrant populations, but certainly some vestiges still exist. A telling accent as in one associated with an Eton or Harrow man versus one of an East Ender renders a powerful effect.

The mother was extraordinarily strict with regards to behavior and attention to schoolwork. She carefully monitored and controlled all of her daughter's social interactions, or more accurately, inaction. Mother was the all-powerful locus of control in her daughter's life. Mrs. was, therefore, for the most of her early life, a very lonely child. She had no siblings, but eventually, somewhere around the age of ten, was given the chance to go off to boarding school albeit in yet another rural setting, but at least she now had unfettered access to other children. She exhibited some initial signs of defiance, superiority and/or arrogance, but was soon set straight by the headmaster's ruler across the palm of her hand. No longer chafing under her mother's watchful eye, she tended to devote more of her energies to sports at which she excelled rather than her studies although she was unquestionably a bright student. Her mother later moved her to Capital City where she boarded with a family and finished high school. It was there that she discovered her talent for theatrical performance.

She became a member of an acclaimed national theater ensemble and appeared in a number of performances. She was well respected by her peers to the extent that almost a decade after her marriage, when she was on vacation in New York, she ran into an old friend and colleague in the lobby of a theater just before the performance was to begin. The friend, now a well-known director, at the end of the play acknowledged her presence in the audience to all in attendance. Later he invited her to once again join a theater ensemble this time with him in a suburban town in the U.K., but Mr. said no. She had a family, she had a home, she had children, she had a husband. And that, as they say, was the end of that. This happened some forty plus years ago and true enough, at the time, she had young children at home. But it was Mr.'s decision, not hers. Perhaps another time, another place, but score another point for external locus of control.

Back now to that summer when Mr. was still eighteen and the future Mrs., fully three years older than he, performing with the little theatre group and decidedly more sophisticated in the art of how to get what one wants was already working at the bank where Mr. would soon be offered a job. Both he and she tell me that she used the summer vacation departure of his then current girl friend as the opportunity to go out with him and essentially become his new girl. The vacationing girl friend in the Bahamas and her mother got wind of the situation as did Mr.'s mom. All and sundry became upset: The age-old story of the experienced *femme fatale*—an actress no less—seducing the inexperienced young lad.

He didn't stand a chance.

Fast forward three years later when it was time for him to accept a scholarship to a university in the U.K. Mrs. turns up pregnant two months before the departure date! Nothing to be done but for them to quickly marry and take the next ship leaving for England before anyone can spot the baby growing in her belly. And did I mention (I believe I did) that the domineering, controlling, would-be socially superior mother of Mrs. turns out actually to be an unwed mother herself? Talk about your locus of control! Do I even bother to say that except in the case of an out-and-out assault or just plain ignorance, women do not get pregnant by accident! The steps that end with that outcome are tried and true, quite predictably 1, 2, 3.

After university in London and two children, Mr. distinguished himself with a decidedly impressive job with the British Foreign and Commonwealth Office and later as a consultant working on behalf of the U.N. He developed data analysis systems for the governments in countries

TONI M. FORSYTH

as far flung as Norway, the Middle East and Africa. He had a bayonet placed at his throat in 1991 at a checkpoint in Libya and ducked for cover when bombs went off outside U.N. headquarters during a meeting in Beirut. He ate sheep's eyes in Syria and dined with royalty in Saudi Arabia. His clothes were expertly crafted by Savile Row tailors, and his shoes were made in Italy of the finest Italian leather. He had an expense account commensurate with the types of places where he was expected to dine and with the types of clients he was dispatched to court. He served at the pleasure of Her Royal Highness Her Majesty the Queen and it was to her that he was ultimately expected to report. He was her VIP emissary. Hometown boy does good.

A few more details this time, but essentially much the same as before. Perhaps this time around there's a bit more emphasis on the role he played as the good looking male lead on the world stage where Mrs. could play her part. Mr. and Mrs. were stationed in Zimbabwe for 12 years where they lived the life of cricket and squash and drinks at the club—the ridiculous lives of British expatriates that one sees depicted in movies such as *Out of Africa*. They were an attractive couple, no doubt about it. They lived out the script that had been developed and written over the course of the previous century, and they lived it well. More flirtations. More affairs? Don't know for sure, but certainly he grew into the kind of sophisticated, self-assured man to whom women are instinctively drawn, and he became more and more skilled in the art of drawing them in. It came naturally to him. But the universe does not cut you any slack for doing what comes naturally when you have half a brain and you can tell the difference between a couple of afternoon quickies and a relationship that begins to develop based on shared values, mutual respect and a concerted effort to engender mutual trust.

January 28th

Dear Abigail:

Mr. was very obnoxious when he got in the car this afternoon, and I was in no mood for it. "They just have to learn to live within their means. If they can't afford it, then they have to learn to live without. They can't keep begging for money every time you turn around."

I was pissed anyway because I've been acutely aware that our spiritual, emotional, mental connection has been slipping away. I couldn't stop myself and I let him have it. But more about the details of the actual dialogue later. What I want to get to before it trickles away from my conscious mind is the revelation that came later that night when I finally understood that what I had been hearing was him "channeling" her, Mrs. His basic instinctive impulses are generous, kind, warm-hearted, giving—despite his protestations of the "logic" behind his point of view. Hers are more instinctively mean-spirited and miserly. I'd been mulling over in my mind a lot about how much of a theatrical performance perhaps her whole life has been. She has managed to orchestrate a fictional account of herself, and tries to mold everything in life that comes her way to fit into the script that she has written or that was written for her as a child growing up with the world's biggest control-freak of a mother:

- *The fiction that her father died when she was only six months old when the reality is that she is the product of an unwed mother who had an affair with a married man who eventually went back to his wife and family in England.*

- *The fiction that she genuinely won away the high-school-age Mr.'s heart from his more age appropriate girl friend when the fact is that there was nothing "genuine" about it—it's an old carnie trick—distract the mark and pick up the change.*

- *The fact that Mrs. was an older more experienced woman, a product of a life lived in the theater behind and in front of the*

TONI M. FORSYTH

velvet curtain and therefore more sophisticated in the art of
the kind of seduction that works to create a powerful illusion
which can so draw in an audience to the extent that the they
can no longer tell fact from fantasy.

—*Distraught*

Advice columnist Abigail von Nostrum welcomes all inquiries sent to her at this newspaper but regrets that she cannot provide personal responses to individual letter writers.

(I keep having to go back to the details. Why is that?) Necessary analysis in order to get a grip.

*T*know now what his mother saw. I can guess what she felt. I can imagine her distress at seeing her beautiful golden boy being led by the nose (or some other appendage) into a hall of mirrors. And when Mrs.-before-she-was-Mrs. thought he might be slipping from her grasp because he would be leaving to go away to university in England, and because he hadn't really lost his heart to her anyway, and she knew it, she pulled a card from her mother's deck and got herself pregnant and married just in time to leave with him on the next ship before she started to show. Presto change-o—the conjuror's trick, a carnie's trick, the oldest trick in the book employed by women across the ages looking to get away from a stifling, going nowhere life. The ultimate challenge: secure a Mrs. degree executed without a hitch.

Could a young woman from a rural town on a small island be that calculating? You betcha. Locus of control.

So back to the car ride into the city and me starting off by feeling really pissed.

(Is this always just about me, me, me? It is about me, but I also hope that it is more about how we all strive to put just enough spin on the ball so that the pins already set up in their lanes with unwavering specificity, fall in such a way that each one impacts the other according to the player's own master plan. We do have some ability to affect outcomes. We just don't have total control or even "enough" control if enough means not ending up with outcomes that just plain suck. Most of us manage to rack up quite a few of those of the course of our lifetimes.)

Mrs. recently decided to go on some kind of "lose 10 pounds in 3 days" diet that she got off the internet. Mr. decided to go on it with her to be supportive. They didn't used to be in each others' space so much. But they are now. I'm angry at her because she's reeling him in, shortening his leash. She's all sweetness and light, but she hardly ever leaves the house on her own these days—maybe once every 5–6 days. She goes in to town with him maybe once a week now. She used to drive herself in every other day. I see her now as being manipulative, and in order for one to be a successful manipulator, one must be good at calculations.

I've never been good at math, so maybe I'm not putting 2 + 2 together and coming up with the right answer with regards to who thinks what. He does have a tendency to want to place blame, to really hit you over the head with it. So when he parroted her words about the helper having to "just have to learn to live within [her] means" it was not in keeping with what I thought was his basic character. Yet he had at one point said that, "it is their fault" (the fault of the island's desperately poor) that that they're not getting by day to day. So maybe Mr. and Mrs. are actually in sync on that one. Maybe he was not just channeling her. They are channeling each other. Birds of a feather.

But if a good relationship is supposed to help one grow, to expand one's consciousness and who one is as a human being—being-in-the-world—then channeling and rehearsing a view of the world that is contrary to what every humanistic philosophy says about what is "right thinking" is also contrary and counterproductive to that which is known to expand who one is as a human being.

If Mr.'s instinctive impulse is to be generous toward his fellow man, then it stands to reason that words uttered that state a position contrary to that impulse are the product of a learned response—a directive from without, not from within. That's her view of the world not his. Maybe that's why I get so mad and want to scream at him, "That's not who you are!

TONI M. FORSYTH

That's not right thought! What are you playing at? You were doing so well, what the hell happened to you? And going along with a 3-day diet taken from off the internet? One-quarter cup beet root, ½ cup string beans, ⅙ cantaloupe or honey dew melon and 4 ounces of tuna? Get real! Get a life! (Or get sick. That'll do it for some real weight loss.)

Voilá! That's it! There it is! The little gray cells, refreshed as they are from a few hours of rest have done their job. The answer has come to me in the night. I know why he has pulled away and Mrs. seems positively joyful. It is because she is. They are. The marriage has been repaired. I have done my job successfully. The job for which, unbeknownst to me, I was hired— to be one arm of a short-sided triangle so that the equidistant arms could continue to hold together. An isosceles triangle. The reason for my employ. Mrs. has had the respite that she needed from her frustrations with him, and Mr. has had the respite that he needed from his frustrations with her. The irritations large and small that had come from over 50 years of living with someone who had manipulated him into a lifelong commitment had dissipated. The pressure had been relieved, the valve reset. They could continue with their cohabitation secure in the knowledge of what had gone before and what was likely to come after. With the prospect of that foreknowledge, there was a certain level of comfort that reigned once again. God's in Her heaven and all's right with the world.

But wait. Could this be it?

Now I must speculate about the reason for the attack (for attack it surely must have been) in the car yesterday! Why out of the blue (seemingly) he was going on and on about people living within, learning to live within their means and not begging for money every time one turns around. I was the beggar! Not Annie the helper who had asked for money and been told off by Mrs. saying that she was done giving handouts and that Annie was not to ever to ask for additional money again. The well was dry, the cookie jar empty. You must learn to live within your means. You must learn not to live above your means. That's why the attack began almost as soon as he was in the car, before we even got out of the driveway.

Many years ago, I had a dear friend Tom, who was the only other person I've ever known with a disposition like mine that has no problem giving money away when we have it, feeling something of an actual obligation or compulsion to do so. While not necessarily deriving an actual sense of pleasure from relieving the distress of others, we are nonetheless driven to satisfy a powerful need to assist our fellow man (or woman or child) when the opportunity presents itself that must—according to our moral code—be met if at all possible. Meeting a dire financial need when asked to do so allows us to exist more comfortably in the world. To whom much is given, et cetera. It is the job of the professional empath to relieve vicariously the experienced anxiety of others and in so doing relieve in turn his or her own unique brand of anxiety. It is unique in that it is at once both internal and external, personal and communal.

But Tom eventually became a paranoid schizophrenic incarcerated in Patton State Prison for the Criminally Insane in San Bernardino, California. The mental disorder was brought on by his single-minded pursuit of recreational drugs in order to party hearty in the gay bars and discos of Hollywood and West Los Angeles. And later, no doubt fueled by the drugs provided from countless clinical trials for which he volunteered during the 1980s and 90s in the hopes of holding the prognosis for his HIV at bay, the onset of full blown AIDS finally took its toll both physically and mentally after the many years of self destructive behavior pursuing the gay nightlife of the times. Must physical and mental destruction be the final destiny of the empath?

> The game is afoot, my dear Watson. Come along. You
> must keep up. There is work to do if we are to avert
> another tragedy.

TONI M. FORSYTH

Does Mr.'s rant about budgeting money somehow reflect upon my profligate charity to the undeserving poor which in turn links me to the self destructive behavior of my friend Tom? From what twisted logic was this line of thought born?

I couldn't understand why my words, just my very presence wasn't disabling Mr.'s weaponry. Why his attack was so sustained and so intractable. It was because it was indirect. It came from the side and from behind. Like his dog, the bitch.

Early on in my tenure here at My Happy Retreat, she bit me once at the back of my right ankle and another time on the side of my left leg. An attempt at equal distribution of services rendered. Like master, like dog? I was traumatized and angry. At the moment, I was all for putting her down, but two years later I ended up saving her life after her master ran over her with his car when he was on his way to an important dinner, running late and wouldn't take the time to stop to see if she were alive or dead or just hurt.

I saved her life.

I went ahead and paid for the services of a vet because in a hurried phone call, Mrs. had told me not to spend any money to keep her alive if her injuries warranted the intervention of a veterinarian. But of course I wasn't going to be responsible for putting someone else's dog to sleep if it could at all be avoided. So I spent the money. Quite a bit. No offer to repay. Frankly, I did not expect them to. I managed to get a small, token amount back at a later date in some kind of routine exchange of goods. Maybe even a little cash involved for the meds but certainly not much.

Daddy used to say, "Money, money, money. The root of all evil." He also used to say, "Poor me, born without a shirt." It seems to me that he said both of those things a lot while I was growing up.

Just spoke with Mr. and asked him if the statements he made about Annie the helper and begging were really directed toward me, and with genuine surprise he said,

"You! Not at all. Why?"

"Because I was asking to temporarily borrow some money to pay the watchman at my house?"

"No, Why do you say that? You're not begging!"

Who's the anxiety ridden paranoid now? But I do feel sometimes as if I'm locked up here at My Happy Retreat in a kind of loony bin.

Turns out, according to him, that I hurt his feelings by even suggesting that he would ever think of such a thing. That if he had his way, he'd take on the oversight of finishing the construction of my house so that I wouldn't have to be plagued by incompetent contractors and cost overruns. I feel bad that I made him feel bad.

Now I feel worse.

Dear Abigail:

Just to let you know that there was no need for me to be pissed. He was actually really, really upset that I could think that he would think that I was "begging for money" (which is what I had interpreted the whole "poor people living within their means" diatribe to be about). He was driving when I called him and he pulled off to the side of the road to set me straight. I felt like a jerk. I had been listening to the old tapes inside my head (my brother) about how I couldn't manage money. The body blow I had felt had not come from Mr. I had delivered it to myself.

—Disturbed

Advice columnist Abigail von Nostrum welcomes all inquiries sent to her at this newspaper but regrets that she cannot provide personal responses to individual letter writers.

TONI M. FORSYTH

I feel the necessity to retrench for a while. I must hunker down. I'm clearly starting to decompensate, to unravel a bit. I discombobulate. I need to regroup. I wonder if I need to stop writing to the disembodied Abigail for direction?

I need to engage in less analysis, draw fewer conclusions and focus more on remembering the wonderful times that Mr. and I spent together, the happy times that cemented our relationship. A thread should develop, a skein, a fabric, a warp and a woof. I'm going to work on that. Is this the telling of the story of Mr. and Mrs. or am I the real protagonist here slowly emerging *sotto voce or basso profundo?* Or perhaps *flagrante in delicto?*

Dear Abigail:

I'm writing because I'm in need of help but I'm not even sure exactly help with what.

—Upset

Advice columnist Abigail von Nostrum welcomes all inquiries sent to her at this newspaper but regrets that she cannot provide personal responses to individual letter writers.

Happiness

*T*urns out the whole Bill of Rights thing in the U.S. Constitution regarding the pursuit of happiness is, in fact, a really big deal. Actually a unique really big deal in the history of the world. Turns out during the course of his life, Mr. never actually thought about being happy. The pursuit of happiness. Never asked himself the question. Am I happy? His whole life!! He belongs to a different generation from mine. A different era. Wow! He's definitely not a Boomer. Also, just read some stuff on line about the Human Potential Movement of the 60's and 70's. It was about self-actualization and the pursuit of happiness. Abraham Maslow and others. As to be expected, Mr. had never heard anything about it. Wasn't part of the curriculum in his British university studies. Today the whole world is talking about and actually studying the concept of Gross National Happiness. How times change.

During the almost year-long exile Mrs. chose for herself when she retreated into the womb-like confines of her home and when she was away visiting her son in Leeds, Mr. and I went out on day-long excursions through the island countryside in search of new sources of seedlings and cuttings for a variety of secondary crops for the estate. We met with small farmers and big plantation owners alike. We drove up into the yards of old estate houses from the 1800's, tiny homes built early in the 20th century and large estate houses built within the last 20 years.

We noted the acquisition over the last decade or two of more and more of the smaller, independently owned farms under the umbrella of a large, island-wide agricultural corporation—a relatively miniature version of the behemoth monopolies that have occurred in first world countries not only in agriculture but particularly in communications—an industry that controls the information that we all receive and that serves to shape our understanding of the world in which we live. We noted the changes that had taken place over the course of our lives not only in the economics but also the social realities of life on the island. We lamented the fact that the movement toward greater mechanization had displaced so many people who had been on their own land and had left the children of those people, and their children's children without the means to sustain themselves and their families.

Mr. and I would drive out mid-morning on Sundays exploring parts of the island that we had not visited since we were children or had never visited before. We stopped in at little museums scattered across the landscape here and there. We got out of the car and marveled at scenic vistas everywhere we turned. But more than anything, we talked and we laughed. We came to appreciate each other's differences in points-of-view and realized, eventually, that there weren't any substantive differences after all. In fact, virtually all of what I had considered to be the more mean-spirited beliefs espoused and positions taken during our early tea time debates were not entrenched in his heart at all. They were the result of intellectual gymnastics—adversarial talking points rallied simply for the purpose of ensuring a spirited conversation. Or maybe for the purpose of keeping his distance, because I came to realize that from early on he had been physically then intellectually attracted to me. In short, over time, we bonded. In the end, we fell deeply in love.

It seemed that every little roadside food court proved to be a "find" of one sort or another. Maybe it really was the food at one particular place that turned out to be exceptional, or maybe it was simply the bamboo growing to incredible heights on either side of the roadway along the route to the location that proved so memorable. Or maybe it was just because for us, at this time in our lives, to have found an emotional connection that both of us independently had long ago abandoned any hope of ever finding made everything so spectacular. Whatever it was, the feelings were overwhelming and only served to highlight for Mr. the emotional sacrifices that he had been willing to make for so many years. In Woody Allen's movie, Crimes and Misdemeanors, there is a character by the name of Professor Levy, a holocaust survivor, who functions as a kind of solo Greek Chorus throughout the plot development. He provides a running commentary on his observations that, for most people, happiness—real happiness—is just not a part of the equation in their lives. In an attempt to achieve it, people spend their whole lives trying to undo or redo childhood relationship traumas with only varying degrees of success.

Both Mr. and myself were trying to undo and redo—him not so much from childhood trauma but from childish stupidity—but for us to sustain the work of both spirit and mind in which we were engaged would be the real challenge. We had forged a new emotional and spiritual reality for ourselves, but circumstances and social pressures would work against us and challenge our perception of what was to be real and what was to be, after all, only an illusion.

Postscript with Irony: It just so happened that one day around noon during one of our trips to the city, the head of that large agricultural conglomerate spotted Mr. and me walking in to have lunch at a restaurant frequented by the Who's Who of Capital City society. He immediately called and reported the siting to his wife, who immediately called and reported the siting to her mother, who immediately called and reported the siting to Mrs. within five minutes of our being seated at the table, Mrs., who already knew, and had broached no objection to the fact that we were driving to the city that day to attend to legitimate business (as always), called Mr. and asked him where he was, what he was doing and reminded him to be "good." Such is the nature of reality in an insular society that can hit you over the head with a cast iron skillet when you least expect it.

TONI M. FORSYTH

Martyrdom As an Interesting Manipulative Tool and As a Recent Development

*S*he has painstakingly developed her character over time such that she has become the martyr to his moods, infidelities, and dalliances.

Now he must do a soft shoe routine if he is to declare his intent to perform the definitive act of absenting himself from the relationship—if, indeed, that is what he wants or even intends to do. I say that, but what else can he do? After so many years, realistically how can either one of them go about repositioning themselves for the *pas de deux* the *denouement?*

With regards to Mrs., what does being a martyr specifically entail? What acts are required, what behaviors are necessary? What particular brand of suffering must one endure? Well, one must stoically put up with the debilitating effects of repeated slings and arrows. Slights and jabs and little body blows to the ego that independently, but certainly cumulatively, result in bright little wounds to one's self esteem. "Why did you do that?" Why did you do it that way?" Why didn't you...?" "You should have...." "You know I like X. Why did you do Y?"

But first and foremost one must put up with spending one's entire life with someone who was not in love with you when he married you and, indeed, would not have married you at all if you had not become pregnant as the result of furtive sexual encounters when the parents weren't looking. One mother was on an extended trip out of the country and had, therefore, left the domicile unattended making the way clear for numerous *rendezvous.*

Another certainly couldn't have been expected to closely monitor the after hours activities of a now officially grown but relatively naïve and still quite young man.

As a woman, to be a martyr one must assume a certain amount of Original Guilt associated with having engaged in premarital sex in an era when the societal pressure against it was absolute. One must also thoroughly embrace the OG associated with following in one's mother's footsteps by getting pregnant out of wedlock and being in the position of having to deal with the panic of trying to figure out what to do next in order to survive the calamity. And one cannot escape the OG that comes from knowing that one cannot fail to recognize the advantages of having hooked up with someone with a very bright future ahead of him who was about to embark on a lifetime of adventure far from the confines of a small island nation. Original Guilt plays a large role in the psyche of the martyr.

As luck would have it, the Universe has ostensibly responded and stepped in to play the saviour of us all. The moral support and physical presence of Mrs. will be needed during the upcoming period of dissolution of their son's 26 year marriage and the pending sale of and imminent departure from the family home in Leeds. Mother's help will certainly be welcomed in order to help with the sorting and discarding and folding and packing. A lifetime reduced to a box. Or boxes. A prelude to her own unraveling. A dress rehearsal as it were.

After the Debacle with Mr. Black (the Door and Window Man)

Mr. assumed an aggressive posture at the very start of our meeting with Mr. Black when he came to the site to receive instructions on the installation of the doors and windows for my house. Mr. Black was half an hour late. Mr. already had a bee in his bonnet owing to the fact that the carpenter from the very beginning of my dealings with him had taken the liberty of calling me by my first name instead of using the more formal and traditional title of Miss or Ms. or even Mrs. It was not only tradition but class consciousness as well that was driving Mr.'s deep sense of offense regarding the issue. But there was additional background noise that was contributing to the profound sense of disquietude.

Mr. began the meeting by pointedly and rhetorically asking the carpenter what time the meeting had been scheduled to begin and commenting on the lateness of the hour and the fact that he had other things to do. Mr. Black mumbled an excuse about having to stop at the gas station but that had he known Mr. was going to be in attendance, he would have been on time. Wrong! Both Mr. and I reacted with stunned silence in the face of such casual disrespect directed clearly towards me, and he immediately went into an aggressive mode of interaction with the witless carpenter for the duration of the time that we spent together. This stance of course did not go unnoticed by Mr. Black resulting in in-kind posturing. Not a pleasant interlude at all.

But the next day Mr. surprised me. He was still angry, and now it was directed squarely at me. He had called me at least twice during the evening after the meeting with Mr. Black with numerous questions about how the carpenter had charged me for his work, whether I had any written record of my payments to him, how did I know I wasn't being cheated in some fashion. I answered his questions as best I could, but I began to realize that those were not really the elements of my dealings with Mr. Black that was driving Mr.'s interrogation of me. Were the questions aimed at trying to discredit the carpenter? To discredit my handling of the business transactions with him? I tried to probe with questions of my own in order to find out what it was that he was really getting at, but I couldn't reach far enough into Mr.'s psyche to get to where I could understand what were his real concerns regarding the clueless carpenter.

So late the next afternoon on the way to inspect the work that had been done during the day, and after telling Mr. about a particularly harrowing phone conversation I had had regarding my bank loan, I asked for two things. First, if he would refrain from sharing my personal business with Mrs. I said I could hear her in the background during some of our telephone conversations providing a running commentary on whatever topic was under discussion at the moment. I didn't like it for all kinds of reasons. He agreed. I then asked if he would not be aggressive toward Mr. Black as he had been the day before. That did not go over well. Once on site, he kept his distance during my review of the day's work. But immediately upon our departure the hapless carpenter was replaced by the hapless lover. He didn't see that any real work had been done, where were the doors? (One set already had been installed, some were leaning against a wall). Mr. didn't see them. "There they are." said I pointing to them in the growing distance as we drove away. But "Where are the windows?" said he. Once again it became clear that this was not really a discussion about windows and doors. And this on top of the nonsense with the bank.

What did he want from me?

The conversation on the drive back to My Happy Retreat soon devolved into my begging him to tell me what the problem really was, what

TONI M. FORSYTH

he really wanted from me. Nothing. I told him that I had spoken to Mr. Black about not calling me by my first name because we were in a work situation. Yes. Mr. Black now understands. I told Mr. that I now felt a rift between us and I didn't want that. It didn't feel good. I didn't want us to part for the evening with this left hanging between us. I asked him not to go until he felt that whatever issues he had were addressed. I told him that what I heard him saying was that I should not allow myself to be disrespected by letting a tradesman call me by my first name. That when I introduce myself to someone who could not be considered a peer that I should say I'm "Miss" and provide only my last name, not first name followed by last name. Don't give away my Christian name. That I must be more alert to my elevated status when dealing with people from a lower socio-economic class.

These things are important to him. That's the way things are done here in this post-colonial island paradise. Mr. is a man who came of age in times past. But what the hell? Honest-to-God, I sobbed. He asked me not to do that to him. To HIM! MY sobbing! MY pain! To HIM! [You know, dear reader, that's part of a particular kind of behavioural pattern.] But I'm telling you, that's not who he is. Inside. Or maybe there's something I still don't understand.

He can't bear to see me upset. He wants to know what he can do. I tell him I am hungry, that there is nothing I want to eat at home and that I would like cheese and crackers. He tells me to come over to the house and that he will fix me cheese and crackers and a cup of tea. I take some time alone in the car to compose myself and then walk over to the Great House. He brings me cheese and crackers and a dinner roll spread with garlic paste and places a pot of tea on a wooden tray covered with a white cloth napkin. Mrs. comes out a few minutes later with peanut butter and offers me cake and ice cream then sits down and joins us on the veran-

dah. Later he walks me home and tells me that he prefers seeing me like I am at this moment. Smiling. Happy.

What an ordeal.

What he has repeatedly given me in a hard, often unkind, topsy-turvy world is a soft place to land. What I have given him in a flat line existence is joy. When all is well, we make each other happy. Very, very happy. Ignore the other. My God, have I gone off the rails?

Comes the Dawn

The scales have been removed from my eyes. The veil has been lifted from my face. The truth has been revealed in the blinding light of day: A touch of narcissism at play here? (The same goes for her). Maybe not clinical narcissism but certainly the term is worth a mention. How about simple self-centeredness? That goes down a bit easier and is probably closer to what's really going on. Women cannot resist his looks and charm. He knows it. He lives his life everyday with this in mind and does, at times, respond in accordance with that reality. This is how he sees himself, and it forms the basis for how he chooses to act in certain circumstances. Not all the time, but certainly, it would appear, some of the time. Unfortunately, however, this is indeed the basis upon which—how many? most? some?—women choose to interact with him.

I have now come to understand that the casual flirtations are an established pattern, a mode of interacting, a way of being-in-the-world that has manifested itself throughout his entire life. His responses are not just a one-off. He engages with the women he meets knowing that they find him attractive and want to be in his orbit. What keeps him and Mrs. together is that she cooks, cleans, provides sex and allows him to have women as friends on the side. He in turn provides respectability (to an illegitimate child that's very important), world travel, an ample roof over her head, food on the table and an attractive man that she can pretend wants her for who she is rather than for just what she can give him by way of a live-in maid who allows him to continue to be ostensibly available while not being actually available. But he is also incredibly loyal. Admirably so. He would never abandon her and she knows it. She has said as much. "He will always come back to me," she once said.

In the end, it is a comfortable arrangement. That's why it has worked for over half a century. I had not recognized the scope, the entrenchment, the immersion, the permeation, the true nature of the personality that I had so fully embraced. I actually had a better grasp of her from early on—but not so much of him. I guess I was too blind, too eager, too needy to see. So be it. The quintessential unavailable man. The brief punctuation points of ecstasy followed by the long stretches of utter loneliness and despair are no longer bearable. That is now my bottom line.

Now I must plan my escape.

He will die overseeing the planting of okra. He will die standing out in the blistering tropical sun. She will continue to wither and grow old re-making garments that were purchased decades ago that have holes in them chewed by insects. She will continue to try to disguise the decay with a button or a bow or an appliqué positioned here and there. That is who they are. That is their fate. I wanted to write that they live fundamentally dishonest lives, but is that really true? They certainly know each other's truths after all this time. No illusions there. It is to the rest of the world that they are in a sense fundamentally dishonest, but then, does that really even matter? Don't we all present a false face, a front so that others see and come to know only that which we want them to know, the illusion that we create, the pleasing picture that we paint if we actually give a damn about what others think.

So, Mrs. again. An interesting new representation of the miserly, niggardly, resource-hoarding crone who does not want to share. (Am I being too hard on her? Will I be punished for being not nice?)

I've allowed myself to be dragged by him into a community based, business and high school partnership, civic engagement math and science project. I am co-chairing it with him. In a supporting role, she agreed to make contact with a few business heads that she knows in order to press for donations. She volunteered to approach a businessman whom she characterized as handsome (though not as handsome, she proclaimed, as Mr.) and who is also a widower. I wanted to see him for myself. I want to be able to cultivate my own network of future contacts and not have to rely on other people to do the networking for me the next time around. I also now realize that I need to meet men who may actually be available for a real relationship. (Is my professed undying infatuation wavering?)

Mr. and I made the rounds yesterday delivering what are essentially begging letters requesting donations from local businesses, banks and one hotel where we had made initial contact two days before. This morning Mrs. calls me and says that she wants to maintain her own contacts and because of her prior relationship with the handsome businessman, she should be the one to pass on any correspondences to him since she is the one who would be the most likely to get a donation from him. She did not want me to even simply drop off the request for donations letter to his place of business since I might screw things up.

In other words, don't go to see the handsome businessman. He belongs to her. Very interesting. I explained to her that I would just be hand delivering the letter that actually should have accompanied the materials that she had given him a few days before. In addition, I, as the lead person in the project, needed to introduce myself and forge my own relationships with potential donors, and she could continue to be the go-to person. She wasn't happy and mumbled something about not being able to go with me today, but could go the following day. But of course I went today because I have another commitment tomorrow and he needed to get the letter in time for his HR Department's meeting this afternoon. I delivered the letter and Mr. Businessman came out to accept it. I told him the facility was impressive. He gave me a map of the buildings and grounds to explore on my own, and we parted ways. I believe I did the right thing. I believe I did not jeopardize the viability of a potential funding source. I believe she was out of line. Was I? I don't think so. Let's see how I feel tomorrow.

Today it's pumpkins. Or is it squash? Mr. just called to inform me that one of the workers has stolen 100 pounds of pumpkins (or squash) and that the police have been called and will be here tomorrow morning to arrest him. (He wanted to share this important news of the day with me.) On another note but tangentially related, unless he reduces the asking price for the plantation, he will drop dead in the pumpkin (or squash or okra or papaya) patch.

I am the comic relief on the triangular stage. I am also, most likely, the designated antagonist over at the performance in the main theater. And though it may be fun to have pretty thoughts about finishing the building of my grand house and the two of us hosting wonderful soirees there complete with grand piano, his actions show that he is a man of familiar patterns, a man of the status quo. Over the course of his lifetime the pattern has repeated itself: dalliances and adultery, followed by spousal outrage, followed by recriminations, followed by promises of fidelity, followed by more dalliances of varying stripes. It's worked for more than half a century. Patterns are familiar. Patterns are comfortable. Patterns are sometimes impossible to break. Indeed, if it ain't broke, why fix it?

Next up: When do I tell him? Tell him what? What do I think I should tell him?

Follow-up: The Businessman wasn't handsome; I'm not interested; I didn't really think I would be. Although, I guess you never know. Nothing beats a trial but an error. At least it shows that I'm still willing to explore options. Next!

TONI M. FORSYTH

The Sun Also Rises (and Sets)

I still keep coming back to the notion that their marriage is built on a foundation of dishonesty, deception and disrespect. But it's their very own home grown crop of dishonesty, deception and disrespect. I've known all along that I've been complicit in all three, but the latter came home to bite me in the butt today.

A few days ago, Mr. and I scheduled time for ourselves to go and see the owner of a restaurant that we had previously secured as the venue for the civic-engagement event that we've been planning. It turned out that she would not be available that day and after e-mailing her, she indicated that Monday would work better for her. I informed Mr. on Thursday, and reconfirmed with him on Friday and Saturday.

As I indicated earlier, the math and science event that Mr. and I have been working on was totally his idea from the get-go. He dragged me into organizing it and eventually, to a very limited extent, Mrs. as well. The coordination, organizing and mistress of ceremonies routine is essentially the kind of thing that I used to do professionally for my academic colleagues, but this time it would be for a community based audience. The day of the event itself would essentially be a walk in the park for me, but from the beginning I knew that the groundwork would be daunting since I did not have the kind of network of contacts that I had when I did it for a living. I agreed to be involved 95% for Mr. and 5% for me. I've done 90% of the groundwork so far: 100% of the written materials including the time spent composing and revising them and dollars spent on printing costs, 99% of the gasoline used to meet with prospective participants and donors, and 95% of the sweat equity in trying to make it a reality. (If the numbers don't add up, I think I mentioned before that I'm no-good at math.)

We spent Sunday evening (yesterday) sitting at a bar in a restaurant overlooking a small cove. Azure blue water. DJ'd love songs from the 60's, 70's and 80's in the background. R&B. Romantic as you can get. Later on a live band.

When we first sat down, I mentioned about going to see the owner of the venue that we'd be using for the upcoming event the next morning. We'd talked about going to see her earlier that very same day and also the day before. Mr. says that oh, by the way, he couldn't go after all because he would be going with a friend to see about procuring some horse manure. No kidding. I became very angry very quickly. I immediately felt disrespected. But the energy behind the disrespect had been building up. He frequently doesn't call me when he says he's going to call me. He frequently doesn't stop by when he says he's going to stop by. I am totally the Other Woman with all the second-class citizenship and cheap behaviour on my part that that entails.

I've been allowing myself to make out with a married man while seated in a car pulled over to the side of the road, parked at some scenic look-out point in the hills—behaviour so humiliating and pathetic as to certify me in my own mind as being downright despicable. Teenage antics. "Get a room" stuff. I've placed myself in the position of sitting around waiting for him to decide when and where we can make love—which is almost never anymore because, I think, he is too afraid of getting caught. (I'm guessing.) And, of course, he's got to be still sleeping with his wife at least once in a while so he's getting **his rocks** off so what's the problem? I told him that so off-handedly chucking his previous commitment to me was disrespectful. He said that it wasn't. I said that it was. I asked him if accompanying his friend to get the horse manure specifically the next day was all that important. I was thinking that perhaps it must really be a big deal in order for him to be able to so cavalierly disregard his promise to accompany me to attend to business associated with a project that he initiated and that he roped me into. I reiterated that blowing me off was patently disrespectful and that he needed to call his friend and cancel and reschedule. He said he would call in the morning.

We went on to have an incredible evening together. Very, very romantic. I asked the DJ to play some Al Green. We sipped exotic rum drinks with little umbrellas in them. We danced. We kissed occasionally and held hands the whole time. Towards the end of the evening and just before the band started to play, we were unexpectedly greeted by the owner of the restaurant/bar, whom Mr. knows, and after a brief conversation was promised the owner's support for and involvement in our project. I thought "The Force" was certainly with us that night.

Comes the dawn. The next morning, I call Mr. 20 minutes before we're supposed to leave to meet with the owner of the event venue, and—surprise, surprise—Mr. says he's going with his friend to get the horse manure!

What can I say other than that I railed on and on at him about the utter lack of regard that he had for me—I said it was abominable conduct on his part, he said it wasn't—and the fact that I'm not a doormat like Mrs. and will not accept being treated this way. He said that we could go to our meeting in the afternoon after lunch. (Who knew what time he was really likely to return?) I told him I was going to call his friend and tell him about his prior agreement to accompany me. He said go ahead. I did and his friend said the matter was between me and Mr. and I agreed, but that I was just letting him know. (Why? To let his friend know what a jerk Mr. was/is?) The end. Except to say that this is not a good sign (one of many?). It does not portend well for the future. How is this breach not worse than the carpenter, after showing up half an hour late, saying that if he had known Mr. would be at the meeting he would have been on time? In other words, it is o.k. to be late for an appointment with me (woman?) but not o.k. to be late if Mr. (man?) is going to be there. It's o.k. to stand me up because I'm only the Other Woman, not his good buddy.

If he'll do it with you, he'll do it to you. He's been a serial philanderer his whole life. He has lied to and deceived his wife for more than half a century! Except she knows about his various affairs (my guess is not all), so maybe it doesn't count as deceit after all. What she got was the (illusion of) respectability that comes from being the wife of a man from a good family who went on to have an outstanding career (she the illegitimate child of a rural postmistress who in turn got herself knocked up by a married boyfriend who was about to dump her when he went off to university), and he got a woman who has such little self respect and such a warped sense of self-esteem (reality) that she repeatedly allows herself to be lied to and deceived all the while professing publicly that she wouldn't put up with such behavior. What hypocrites! What a crock! But what the hell does it all say about me? I know only too well.

How do I step away from all of this pathology? Quickly? Slowly? I feel sick.

July 7th

*S*trange. I'm beginning to feel an allegiance to Mr. only when I'm experiencing an immediate connection to him. And I only feel connected to him when we've spent some meaningful time together. The connection is getting harder and harder for me to maintain especially because there has been very limited physical intimacy between us. His choice, not mine. We had a "make-out session" by a swimming pool at a beach house last week, but once again, I felt despicable and cheap afterwards. It's as if I'm some floozy that he's getting a few easy thrills off of. I sense that I may be coming closer and closer to phoning Mrs. and letting the cat out of the bag.

I think I may do it as much out of spite than anything else. Spite towards him for not maintaining the connection. Spite towards her for the little stunt she pulled in pre-op just before his routine diagnostic medical procedure. Calculate my options here. What are the consequences for me if I do spill the beans? Tension on the home front. What if I'm told to leave the premises? If I am told to leave, I can take my time because they can't put me out on the side of the road. They could move to evict me. That would definitely take a few months if not forever. He wouldn't. Not in a million years. I know that. Don't be so dramatic.

I'm going to run this decision past my dear friend whose is coming to visit from the States. She's arriving at the end of the week. Mr. has been very non-committal about going with us to visit my cousin on the other end of the island for a couple of days next week. If he doesn't go, that pretty much seals his fate. I'm going to call Mrs. from the road and tell her. Let him deal with it when I'm not around. As of now, I think I'm going to let him know in advance what I'm going to do. I'll tell him on Sunday after breakfast. Then again maybe I will tell her the day before I leave on the trip just so I can stick around long enough to see what the fallout is like. Woman scorned!

Yes, I'm angry. No two ways about it. I figure that I don't have much to lose by now because the loving feelings I've had, I feel them slipping away. He's allowing them to die. You have to keep stoking the fire otherwise it burns out. I'm going down not in flames but in sackcloth and ashes.

A Slow Death, A Life Without Joy

*H*is marriage to her all but kills that which is best in him. It suffocates his spontaneity, his natural generosity and the goodness in him that are at the heart of his life affirming impulses. All that I think is best in him.

He carves out his domain with his workers and he practices his benevolence with them and says to her, "You let me handle my men around the property, and you can handle the household help." So she is miserly and penny-pinching and not particularly liked by the women that I have known who have worked for her inside the house, and his men do not like it when she is left in charge. They doggedly long for his return on the rare occasions in the five years that I have known him when he was able to break free of the grinding demands of the plantation and fly away to freedom from the grind for a brief time.

About a year ago—just before I became so heavily invested in our relationship—we were sitting in the car having just returned from a day-long trip to the city and he spontaneously turned to me and said, "You have brought joy into my life." And it dawns on me now that what I see is that his marriage to her, on a daily basis, sucks the joy out of his life because there is no breath of air, no spark of life or flash of light working its way through the windows of their existence. The doors to the Great House are both figuratively and literally shut except for brief periods here and there throughout the course of the day.

Does she have something on him that makes him stay? Is it guilt? Over what? The first big affair when he truly fell in love for the first time in his life? She was at home alone taking care of two little kids, and he was eagerly exploring what it meant to be fully himself and fully free, exploring his sexuality, living in Norway on his own—well not quite on his own as it turns out. Or was it over the second big affair when he was left on his own in the Great House for a little over a year and the lure of romantic nights at a luxury hotel with a beautiful and electrifying woman emboldened and energized him such that he brought the woman into his home that was without its resident mistress at the time? Sounds like a Harlequin Romance, and yet....

But now, once again, the reality of his life has slowly crept in and I see there is no longer any joy. That's what I'm seeing in him now: a man who is slowly being desiccated from the inside out. When he is with me, when he is able to break free, he is so different. There is constant giggling and laughter and repartee and engendering of new ideas and flashes of insight and stimulation of the senses and revelations about who we are as individuals and who we are as ourselves together. But day after day caught in the suffocating routine of that house, of cups of tea at 5 pm, of the evening feeding of the dogs, of the watering of the plants in the pots on the verandah, of the banal chatter-of-her, the hum, hum, hum of her like a never ending drum beat on the brain—day after day it takes its toll.

And this is what I'm seeing. What I feel in his slow withdrawal from me into himself is his withdrawal from the warmth and purpose of the life that he and I share, and I feel hurt and confused and abandoned. And I know that sometimes he retreats into himself and into a fantasy of what our life could be like in the house that I am building. That's why he doesn't want me to give it up. He sees in it the possibility of his own freedom, a life meant to be lived, a joyful life for him as well.

What I have come to believe is that he cares deeply about me but that he's stuck—again I don't fully understand why unless it is simple guilt, or perhaps not so simple but a complicated guilt, or perhaps straight-up loyalty and a profound sense of commitment to an oath he took barely as a grown man but barely out of his adolescence that keeps him living a semi-somnambulant, half dead, half awake existence. Once upon a time a twice-weekly game of tennis helped to energize him, keep him feeling alive, but the nearby court closed and that source for release and relief has been gone for almost two years now.

I don't like her for doing this to him. But isn't it true that he is choosing to do it to himself? He is so much more. Maybe my purpose in life is to free him with a thunderbolt, a lightening strike. And then what? Am I meant to go down in flames for attempting it? In the end, am I meant to be punished? To be banished? To cease to exist? Would he even move forward if given the chance to be free or would the comfort of routine bring him round once again to that which he has come to expect and accept: A life without joy?

"My Woman"

*H*ave I mentioned anywhere yet that from time to time he refers to me as "My Woman" or "His Woman?" If I haven't, and I don't think I have, then I know I haven't mentioned what an absolute turn-on it is for me. Ten, twenty, especially thirty years ago to be any man's "Woman" was to be his subservient, his possession. It would have been anathema to the sensibilities of any feminist. It would have meant he had ownership of me and that, to the enlightened mind, meant a kind of slavery, an abdication of personal responsibility, a surrender of one's God-given human dignity and personal freedom.

But now what it means to me is that I belong to someone in a good sense—in the best of all possible senses. A *couple* of weeks ago he asked a mechanic at a gas station if there was anywhere nearby where we could go for a drink. Apparently the man must have pointed to a dive nearby because Mr. came back to the car saying, "I told him I can't take My Woman there."

A clear declaration of ownership. I now "belong" to a man. There is somebody in a position of authority and strength and standing who is looking out for me, who cares about what happens to me, who is concerned about my receiving the respect that he actually thinks I deserve, who feels tasked with my safety and security and well being. That's powerful stuff. I've always been told that I needed to be able to do that for myself; that it would have been despicable weakness on my part and a moral affront to the sensibilities of decent people everywhere for me to expect somebody else to assume that responsibility; that there was absolutely nobody else who would want to or who ought to take on that burden. And make no mistake, burden it would have been. For me to posit the alternative would have meant to acknowledge a fundamental corruption, a primal moral failing at my very core (which has always been suspect anyway).

For him to call me his Woman brings tears to my eyes because it means that for the first time in my life I can relax a bit. I don't have to struggle so hard. I can stop for a minute and catch my breath. It's powerful stuff to be somebody's Woman. It takes a bit of the edge off. It means I belong. It means I'm not alone.

P.S.: I shared this little essay with Mr. I think he liked it. He smiled.

Busy Work

*M*r. and Mrs. have both learned how to sublimate their feelings and retreat into their own little worlds of busy work. She does light housework, mindlessly singing to herself and lightly dancing about the kitchen listening to music on the radio while he thinks up which new crop he's going to plant in order to bring in a little extra money. Okra. Wait. Been there, done that. Something new. Carrots. Hmmmmm.

She mends clothes that have been sitting around for twenty years or more. Some of them are decades out of style, some much too youthful for an elderly woman pushing 80, now starting to stoop when she walks. Clothes that have been ravaged by time, sitting in a closet in the tropical heat subject to the vagaries of the appetites of various moths, beetles and other bugs searching in the dark, damp corners of closets and folds of clothing looking for their next meal, their next tasty tidbit. She sews on a decorative button here, a bow or piece of ribbon there—anything to try and disguise the holes with the ragged edges, the frayed remains of fabric where tiny pincers have had their way with delicate threads of silk and cotton and wool, the warp and the woof dismantled from their original tightly woven web.

Isn't that just like the lives that Mr. and Mrs. live? She at times seemingly mindless, he more or less ambitionless, both of them stuck marking time in the darkened interior of the 18th century Great House. He of the fine mind, she of the mind less and doesn't mind. It actually boggles the mind. Why has he chosen to stay with her? And why is he repeatedly just casually straying never quite enough to break free? How could any of it ever have been enough? Was it just not enough? He who I see as brave, in charge, in command, in control. He who had a knife to his throat while visiting as a U.N. representative in a Middle Eastern country torn by sectarian strife yet lived to tell the tale. He who ate sheep's eyes in order to fulfill his role as Her Majesty's unflappable emissary, in order to dine with the sheik.

To me he is "Bwana." (Have I talked about this before? I can't remember.) Yes, ridiculous, something out of Kipling, something out of "Gunga Din." And yet, here at My Happy Retreat, here in the heart of this little hillside village where the three of us live—Mr. Mrs. and Me; here where the remains of the last remnants of the much larger estate that was the original far-as-the-eye-can-see My Happy Retreat still exists; here where local men actually come to him to settle disputes, cutlasses in hand ostensibly ready to do battle over some indignity, some trespass imagined or real; here where a grandfather comes with babe in arms saying that the Baby-mother, herself a child, has run off and will Mr. "give me a money" to feed the babe or will Mr. ask the lady who lives on the property—Me—if she will take the baby and care for her for a day, a week, a month, a year, forever.

This too is busy work. While Mrs. is upstairs stitching up or letting out the latest seam, the latest hem, he is making decisions that will affect the lives of other human beings age 17 months to 70 years and beyond. He is also deciding whether to plant squash, or cucumber or papaya or okra. He is deciding whether to buy a horse on a whim or go out to coffee or lunch on any given day with his erstwhile friend—Me.

We like to go to places that are right on the water—the café on the upper level of the tourist centered duty-free shopping village near where the huge cruise ships dock that sells the special coffee beans and makes a wicked brew to drink at a moment's notice; the open air restaurant on the beach next to the government office where he invariably has a bowl of conch soup (it's supposed to be an aphrodisiac—as if he needs that to stoke his libido!); the beautiful hotel on the beach where I spent so many wonderful vacations with my 97, 98, 99 year-old mother who was in a wheel chair; the restaurant and bar where the lights are positioned under the surface of the water and are turned on at dusk and a live band plays on Sunday nights.

Common Cause

*W*e click on so many levels. Our interests are so much the same: our intellectual pursuits, our love of the tropical landscape of our homeland, our appreciation for the myriad of architectural styles of so many beautiful homes built over the centuries of the many phases of the island's development—Georgian, gingerbread, Mediterranean, modern. We cared for and about each other, and the compelling call to attend, in one way or another, to the welfare of our impoverished brethren was always in our hearts.

At one point, about four months after my stint in the Miami hospital ER due to my anxiety induced heart problems, Mr. boarded an airplane to fly with me back to Miami in order for me to see a bunch of different doctors and take a bunch of tests. (Yes! Mrs. approved the trip!) We visited with and stayed for two nights at the home of a woman who had been a colleague and dear friend of mine. She and her husband treated us with incredible hospitality and kindness. She is the one who told Mr. and Me about the math and science project involving local high schools and businesses that she had been working on in her community. The idea sparked the desire in Mr. to do the same kind of thing when we returned home to Paradise Island. What eventually developed into his passion for re-creating the project back home became my willing mandate for execution. We were excited to have my friend, who had now become our friend, come and stay at My Happy Retreat for a week and participate as a Featured Speaker in our version of the math and science project. Mr. and I planned for weeks where we would take her and what we would all do when she arrived. "Wait until Friend comes," we would say. We could hardly wait.

Would Mrs. join us in our excursions? She would be invited, but let's wait and see what happens.

A Narcissist?

(An excerpt from the Notes of Dr. Peterson)

Some individuals think they are great and special people who should be admired and respected by others. Such people are often called "narcissists." The term narcissism comes from the mythical Greek character Narcissus, who fell in love with his own image reflected in the water. In the extreme, narcissism can be a clinical disorder [1], however, it is also widely studied as a personality trait in non-clinical populations [2]. The narcissistic personality is characterized by inflated views of the self, grandiosity, self-focus, vanity, and self-importance [3]. Narcissistic individuals have an exceptionally positive view of themselves, and the narcissistic personality is associated with a complex configuration of intrapersonal and interpersonal outcomes [4].

Citation: Konrath S, Meier BP, Bushman BJ (2014) Development and Validation of the Single Item Narcissism Scale (SINS). PLoS ONE 9(8): e103469. doi:10.1371/journal.pone.0103469

*T*his a legitimate query. I admit there's some name-calling, some labeling implied, but nonetheless, the question looms as if in a balloon loitering over my head as I try to craft the direction of my emerging train of thought.

Does referring to someone as a narcissist require that they meet the strict clinical definition of the term or can someone who is just more or less a self-centered jerk also qualify? Maybe the key to the answer lies in recognizing the "would-be" narcissist based on what he or she actually does that embodies certain salient features that resemble narcissism. Does a narcissist—would-

TONI M. FORSYTH

be or otherwise—consciously choose to latch on to vulnerable people, or is it that they latch on to him? Or her? Or maybe they all just latch on to each other like magnets despite the random nature of chance encounters, and based on the peculiar circumstances of each individual, those people become co-dependent upon one another. Then they can all exploit one another for their own ego driven purposes.

The deliberate intentions of the narcissist may not be diabolical, but the disastrous results can be the same as if they had been. The actions of this personality type can sometimes seem quite cruel, causing great pain to those from whom they seek gratification. It is upon that gratification that they must must constantly feed, so that they can carefully determine, in any given instance, what particular helping hand needs to be offered and generously given—a veritable glut of generosity—so that the image of themselves is clearly reflected in the eyes of the victim. And the image is a beatific one indeed! And when the narcissist is at last satiated by the reflection of his or her face in the eyes of another, he or she begins to withdraw back into the inner world they inhabit. Of what? Self satisfaction? Self congratulation? Existential euphoria?

Some people manage to hang on in relationships with a self-absorbed partner for decades enmeshed in the drama of it, having essentially sold their souls to the devil for what they perceive to be the greater reward as I believe we can see in the relationship between some wives and their husbands. The wife closes her eyes to one affair after another or closes her ears to his intemperate words directed at her if he is annoyed about some minor malefaction on her part. In that case, the husband is the narcissist seeking in the eyes of each new lover the perfect vision of himself enthralling and eminently desirable. He sees his wife's petty domestic flaws—perhaps her seemingly unfocused activities, lack of attention to detail (in his eyes), slighting of certain procedural approaches to household tasks—as an affront to his finely honed sense of order, right thinking and right action. In his eyes she comes to embody a disruption to the rational order of things: a breach in the fabric of rationality itself. The wife endures the role of victim closing her eyes to the infidelities that abound and accepts each reproach because she has bought into the conceit of general acclaim he enjoys as well as his own self-image and considers herself lucky to be able to bask in the afterglow of his luminescence.

Or some people can hang on for years in a kind of back and forth with an employer with narcissistic tendencies. We see it in the case of the over-qualified-for-the job alcoholic employee, feverishly pursuing his personal demons all the way down to the last drop at the bottom of a bottle of rum while the former, fulfilling the role of co-dependent, repeatedly bales him out of debt at the local bar. The employer puts up with the weekend binges and late Monday morning appearances because he has in this particular worker a man far too intelligent and far too competent and way over qualified for the back breaking labouring work that his addiction has driven him to endure in order to put food on his table and another drink under his belt. In this case, the employer gets to both complain and pat himself on the back at the same time for being such a wonderful fellow for continuing to employ the drunkard, and basks in the glory of his own munificence. Meanwhile, the employee gets to sink further and further into his addiction because his disease has been enabled by the person who steadfastly continues to put up with his self-destructive behaviour.

Or there are some people who eventually may be forced into fleeing from a toxic relationship with a narcissist in a cloud of *sturm und drang* as in the case of the woman with a young son who begs for her married paramour to leave his wife and marry her at least for her son's sake if not for hers. But in at least one unique instance, unlike others where the narcissist has gotten to parade in the glory of his reflection and seen the Other Woman tremble with eager anticipation in the presence of his great light, in this one instance the victim proves to be no victim at all. She manages to rally her own sense of self worth when her lover fails to follow through on his promises and she eventually sees him for the ultimately self-serving, self-absorbed person that he is and exits in her own blaze of glory.

...conventionally translated as "Storm and Stress"...a proto-Romantic movement in German literature and music taking place from the late 1760s to the

TONI M. FORSYTH

early 1780s, in which individual subjectivity and, in particular, extremes of emotion were given free expression in reaction to the perceived constraints of rationalism imposed by the Enlightenment....

http://en.wikipedia.org/wiki/Sturm_und_Drang-cite_note-1

Or some people end up being kicked to the curb as is the case in the heart wrenching abandonment of a naïve and open-hearted, young girl who falls for an exotic looking young man from a far away land while he works on assignment in her homeland for months on end cut off from the watchful eyes of his wife and young children.

Then there are the others who simply perish willy nilly by the wayside as the narcissist carries on, to varying degrees, his or her casual pursuit of seeing in other people the means by which to admire his own reflection and serve his own ends in the mirror of their gaze. For all of us who manage to let go of our relationship with the narcissist for whatever reason—either by conscious choice or by forced disengagement—the frightening prospect is that we end up disengaging because of the disintegration of the very fabric of our being due to the tearing and shredding and utter annihilation of the self that is who we are.

The narcissist swallows us whole. Like Lot's wife we defy the ban and turn our eyes towards where we dare not look. I cast my gaze, and he casts his, and one of us is totally and utterly consumed in a pillar of salt.

You descend from time to time into a kind of nether world where I cannot reach you—you who seem to be so much the other half of me, the other half of my being, the other half of my mind, the other half of my soul—you go away somewhere, and I cannot even see in your eyes the place to go where to find you, the spot to search in order to seek you out because you have so thoroughly disappeared from the grasp and the reach of my heart.
Where are you?

He systematically opened me up like a can of sardines, painstakingly winding back the lid to reveal the tightly packed tender morsels of flesh within. When we were driving back and forth along the freeways skirting greater Miami going to endless doctor's appointments and never ending lab tests, he told me "I want you to tell me everything. Everything. I want to know everything about you. Don't hold anything back. I want to know it all. Have you held anything back? Have you told me everything? Are you sure? What else? You can tell me. It's okay. I just want to know. Just tell me." I was reeled in like an exhausted deep-water fish. I later came to find out that my sister-in-law had told Mr. an enormous pack of lies and distortions of the truth about me, about my two failed marriages, about my daughter, about my supposedly outrageous relationships with a slew of men that never were, and he was testing my historical account of my life and my marriages against the ahistorical fiction that he had been fed, the lies he had been told. But still. The method by which he cross-examined and interrogated me was relentless. Bordering on the abusive. That's what it felt like.

My final analysis? Up until right now, I don't think I fully understood what it would have meant to engage with a true narcissist. If a person is simply self-centered and self-absorbed—far less damning personality flaws—are those sufficient qualifiers for the awful label? But isn't the end result for those with whom they come in contact—the emotional devastation—just about the same?

I, on the other hand, have always been "Other" directed. I empathize with the plight of the Other; I am ready, when I can, to give people money, to help them out financially, to ease the way, to make them less anxious, to make things better for them as best I can. I cannot abide the suffering of others. I cannot sit idly by in the face of someone else's pain if I can at all be of help. That's why I give the maid money for her blood pressure medicine; that's why I gave her the equivalent of $U.S.$200 so her daughter could take her high school exams; that's why I gave her $100 when she needed to pay her rent. That's why I paid for two years of boarding school and for every other single thing the young boy who did chores on Saturdays needed in order to be given a chance to experience a decent education and move beyond his abusive home life. That's why I bailed the high school boy, the part time worker, out of jail and paid $750 for his lawyer and then more money for various court fees. I drove him to his hearings and depositions and court appearances over and over and over again and suffered from the bailiff driving up to my front door yelling at me that I'd be going to jail. I ended up paying a fine of $850 and an additional $250 for my own legal representation when the boy—the young man—didn't show up for court when he was supposed to on the one occasion when I asked him to get there on his own. And two years later the case is still not settled. Maybe I am not just "Other Directed." Maybe I am just a fool.

More Focus on the Other: I wanted to make sure that Mr. saw the doctors he needed to see in order to stay well—the gastroenterologist who did the routine diagnostic procedure (and we know how that turned out with Mrs. barring me from the pre-op consultation) and the ophthalmologist (whom he has yet to see) because he is going to start losing his vision in his left eye, and soon in both due to a small cyst steadily growing in each of them close to the cornea. Pterygia. Isn't that what a loving partner does? Look out for and help to ensure the safety, health and well being of the other? You keep on them until they do what needs to be done. You don't closet yourself away refurbishing your wardrobe, probing the possibilities of a facelift to magically erase away the toll that the years have taken on your ego while totally ignoring your life-support responsibilities to your partner. At least that's what I thought.

Just as he took care of me, I tried to take care of him in the only way I knew how by assisting with the marketing for the sale of his property, by triggering renewed interest in the leasing out of plots of his land, by putting my heart and soul and all my energy into pulling off the community event that was his idea and his obsession and his desire, by making sure he attended to his health. And certainly he seems grateful for what I've done. But yet it also now seems to me as if what he must really want is what he has been used to receiving his whole life long from the women who are the planets that orbit his sun: women hovering over him, bringing him tea and coffee, fixing his meals, ministering to his every need, and providing hours on end of mindless, endless, constant chatter to fill up every nook and cranny of the empty spaces of Time writ large.

Or maybe he is simply able to resign himself to what fate dictates he endure (so unlike me!). Like the sheep's eyes in Syria. It is just not in his nature to take on the Palace Guard. The Queen speaks and he is honour bound to listen and to obey. It is his sworn duty. He serves at the pleasure.

He comes and goes emotionally. Sometimes he sees me, sometimes he doesn't. As of now, I have become invisible, delegitimized. I cannot see into his eyes; my image is no longer reflected there. I willingly cop to the fact that for now I am needy. I am the one who has to have her existence verified through the gaze of another. Who is the real narcissist here?

I could have made sure the coffee and tea were poured and the meals and snacks were prepared if given the chance. If that's what it takes. If that's what he really has to have. What I can never do is provide the hours of endless, constant, mindless chatter that Mrs. supplies in spades. But he and I are capable of spending endless hours and days engaged in really good, really meaningful, really intelligent conversation and intellectual stimulation and laughter and giggles and fun. And also planning for more bridge-building civic-engagement interventions in the community in which we live. Good works. Doesn't that count for something toward my redemption? Isn't that worth the price of all the tea in China?

To be a true narcissist means that during every second of every minute of every hour of every day one has to be obsessing about oneself. It—whatever "it" is—has to be always about that person and how it reflects on him or her. So for instance (and I realize at the time Mr. was freaked out about undergoing a routine exploratory medical procedure when he had never before in his whole adult life experienced anything more than a simple injection), in spite of me providing the use of my more comfortable automobile and accompanying Mr. and Mrs. to Capital City for the procedure, there was no room, no space available in his mind for him to see how I ended up being not only excluded but nullified, de-authorized, rendered worthless, cast out onto the ash heap, cut out from the herd, isolated away

TONI M. FORSYTH

from the pack certainly by Mrs. herself and but also in extension by his family with whom he is very close. They all chose to abandon *en masse* the premises where I was deposited the night before the examination of his internal organs was to take place and rallied to Mr.'s side in his hour of need at his brother's house where he and Mrs. were directed to spend the night. In forgetting about me then, he was not being narcissistic, he was merely being a scared little boy.

The day after the math and science joint venture day, there was to have been a big island-style breakfast for our Friend, the Featured Speaker, at the Great House, but it was cancelled because Mr. was sick. He had developed flu-like symptoms and was taken ill with fever and chills and was holed-up in bed. But wait a minute—the on-site cook was still available. Certainly Mrs. had to eat. The food had been purchased and was sitting in the refrigerator. The guest still had to eat. However, I ended up having to scramble to find a way to provide breakfast for "our" friend, "our" guest, "our" visitor from another country, and in the end, she made suggestions about where to eat and things worked out just fine. I'm just saying, if it had been me, I would have served the breakfast anyway. Everyone still had to eat.

But I was getting sick too. I was experiencing shortness of breath, an albeit less dramatic reoccurrence of my ER symptoms. My heart was pounding, and I was coughing more and more—a newly developing symptom (there would be more, one ultimately life-threatening) in reaction to one of my many medications. The preparations and final execution of the event had taken its toll on me. I needed to debrief with Mr. I wanted to know if he had been pleased with the results of my hard work, if he thought I had done a good job. My anxiety, the bane of my existence, the source of all my angst, was building. I was beginning to feel stress and panic at the thought of having to attend to our guest all on my own.

The doors and the windows to the Great House remained closed to Friend and me. I couldn't get through to him on the phone. Mrs. ran across 100+ yards of open space to collect the Sunday paper we were asked to purchase by Mrs. to bring to him. She ran in order to keep us from approaching the house, from getting too near the sanctuary. Mrs. had now assumed the role of gate-keeper to the crypt—the Crypt Keeper as it were. We had to scramble to make arrangements for dinner as well. After so much planning, there was now no plan.

The next day, Monday, more of the same: the doors and the windows to the Great House were shut when we arose. Exclusion. Friend fixed breakfast for the two of us. Later on, when we were leaving to go out for the day, we saw that the front door to the house was open and we thought, "This is our chance! Let's go see how Mr. is doing."

He greeted us at the door. He was feeling better. We chatted. He asked, "Why didn't you call me on my phone?" to see how he was doing. And I said that I had called his cell phone number several times but there had been no answer. I told him that I had been scrambling to try to provide meals for our friend who had spent $800 out of her own pocket to travel here to be the Featured Speaker at the event two days before that he had engineered and that I had orchestrated. It was his brain child and I had delivered it for him, not for me, but for him because he really, really wanted it to happen, and I really, really wanted to make him happy and to please him because he had made me really, really happy and had pleased me and made me feel so much better about being alive than I had felt in decades.

> *Sometimes we see in our belovéd something that we*
> *think they don't see in themselves, something that we*
> *think they are capable of and wouldn't it be great if they*
> *just went after that thing, and sometimes we want that*
> *thing for them and we so desperately think that they*
> *ought to have that thing and ought to want that thing*
> *the way we want it for them, but they don't want it for*
> *themselves, and sometimes all of the wanting and not*

wanting leaves a lot of frustration lying around on the floor just waiting to trip somebody up. And sometimes somebody does trip, and sometimes somebody does fall, and sometimes somebody does get hurt. Then you've got to figure out what to do to try and fix it, to cleanse the wound, make sure it doesn't fester and make it all better. To make sure somebody doesn't die because of it.

After the Visit

What a mess! The now "Former" Friend who had been "our" guest ended up inserting herself into the lives of people she didn't even know in a most outrageous and oh so destructive way. She took sides, against a husband and wife and intervened in a domestic situation that was not hers in which to intervene, carried tales back and forth between the three parties involved and then flew the coop! Later on a mutual friend said that she had confided in him that she did it to help me. But she didn't help me. She didn't even help her new best friend, Mrs., because Mrs. ended up developing an ulcer and broke out in hives over allegations of the plotting of an impending palace *coup* which, in fact, had never been plotted at all. Fifty-three years of a carefully developed *détente* in the relationship between husband and wife was destroyed and flushed down the toilet in a matter of a few days all in the name of "just wanting to help."

Shiva the Destroyer: (E-Mails to Another Friend About Former Friend)

From: *Me*
To: *Another Friend*
Sent: *Sunday, July 22nd, 11:33 PM*
Subject: *Re: It's Over!*

Dear Another Friend:

O.K. Here goes: I've known Former Friend for 20+ years. She was a colleague of mine from a different college. She assisted me and did presentations at the various conferences and workshops that I produced all across the U.S. a number of years ago. We became really good friends, and Mr. and I spent two days with her and her husband at their home when we were there earlier this year, so she knows the situation involving myself and Mr. He and I had a great time with them.

Fast forward to last week. Mr. had gotten excited about and wanted to create a math and science community engagement project here in Tourist Town loosely modeled after one that had been implemented across the U.S. in which my friend has been involved at a local level. He wanted me to spearhead it here even though I told him that I'm retired and not interested in putting the necessary energy required into doing the donkey work to make it a reality and essentially being the live entertainment as lead facilitator for a day-long event when I'm still struggling with my house issues and my illness.

Bottom line is that I allowed him to drag me into it. And I really did it for him but only because I knew I could use a design model that I had developed years ago, so there was no brain strain in adapting the architecture of it for a new audience. Implementation however was another story just because of how incompetent and ineffectual everything is in this country and how nothing works like it's supposed to in this stupid banana republic.

Enter my now Former Friend who volunteered to purchase an expensive airplane ticket to Paradise Island on her own dime in order to be a Featured Speaker and who actually raised $100 in donated cash for the project. Amazing! The first night she was here, Mr. and Mrs. hosted a dinner at their house for my friend and the Keynote Speaker from the university in Capital City who was going to be doing a reading at the event. I ended up not going for several reasons. #1 is that I think it's damn weird and just plain wrong to be sitting at the dinner table across from my would be lover and his wife who helped prepare and serve the meal. The word **HYPOCRITE** screams out to me in cacophonic, ear splitting decibels, and had I acquiesced to such a demand, it would have been emblazoned in day-glo neon lights across my forehead. #2 is that something went wrong with the internet at the precise moment I was trying to print out enough copies of the materials that were to be handed out to the participants the next morning. I ended up not finishing until 1:30 am as it was. If I had tried to attend the dinner as well, I would never have made it alive. But the upshot was that my friend began to bond with Mrs. and ended up deliberately and inconceivably contradicting a specific request that I had made of Mrs. about participation at the event!

Meanwhile, it turns out that Mr. had picked up some kind of virus and by the next evening was sick in bed with fever and chills. Mrs. closed up the house like Fort Knox. My friend and I were unable to have any contact with Mr. at all because Mrs. became the Keeper at the Gate. She would not let either of us talk to him even on the phone. In the meantime, no longer in quiet desperation, I'm venting to my friend about how difficult it is to be the Other Woman. Here I was concerned about his health and wondering what voodoo brew of native leaves and bark and seeds and roots and herbs Mrs. was trying to give Mr. to try and cure what ailed him and could do nothing to intervene. Eventually, I was able to suggest zinc tablets for his flu-like nasal congestion and ibuprofen—absolutely not aspirin—for the aches and pains. I was also getting mad at him for allowing himself to be isolated like that. I guess I was just plain bad mouthing him even though I knew he was ill, and my friend *took it as the green light to go ahead and launch into a diatribe about what dogs all men are, how her first husband had been a dog who had treated her so badly by running around with all kinds of women, taking all the family assets including her jewelry (24K gold) and ultimately leaving her destitute, and by the way, wasn't Mrs. just such a lovely person?*

This characterization morphed into my now Former Friend then going out of her way to visit with and chat up Mrs. telling her she needed to keep tabs on her man and not let him take advantage of her good nature. The parallel dialogue with me once again centered around what a dog Mr. was for cheating on Mrs., for taking advantage of my fragile, vulnerable state and that I was to move away immediately from My Happy Retreat home of almost 5 years and never have anything to do with him again. The fact that Mr. was not in love with Mrs. when he married her, is not in love with her now and indeed had never ever been in love with her (with her acknowledging as much to be the case!) was irrelevant. Sticking with her for fifty+ years out of a sense of duty, loyalty and simply not wanting to hurt her was all well and good, but he needed to man up and suck it up for the next fifty+ years because Mrs. is such a lovely person.

The denouement to this little drama occurred on the day Former Friend was leaving. I had told her I would drive her to the airport. Originally, Mr. and I were to drive her, but since he and I had been estranged over the last several days because I felt that he had allowed himself to be wheedled out of pulling his fair share of the entertaining duties (Remember: WE not ME had made all kinds of plans for entertaining her during her visit), he was making noises that he would not be going to the airport ostensibly because he was still sick. I knew he had been sick, but he was better. He had pulled his usual disappearing act into himself. It didn't have all that much to do with his illness but more to do with—I actually haven't figured out yet exactly what it has to do with. Maybe he was punishing me for not being at the dinner on the first night that he had insisted I attend. Maybe he was still just nursing the remains of his virus.

(Dare I say I realize that some men have a tendency to pull themselves into their caves when they are sick and not feeling up to facing the challenges of the world, and they remain there until they are once again what they consider to be their old virile selves?

Maybe it's a prehistoric survival thing. But of course women don't have that luxury because the children have to be fed and dinner has to be made! When the older women can no longer hack it, there are always younger ones ready to come along and take up the slack.)

I digress. Departure day. Friend was insisting that I should not drive her to the airport but that she should take a coach/bus. I know what she didn't want was for me and Mr. to have time together alone in the car on the way back home. She wanted me to dump him and never have another word to say to him in this lifetime or the next. These were the sentiments (if not actually stated in so many words) that she had been expressing to me during the intervals when she was not indoctrinating Mrs. with the lectures specifically prepared to address her circumstances vís a vís Mr. But I equally insisted that as the hostess it was my responsibility to see my guest off properly. I would drive no matter what.

Come the morning of departure, and as I am getting dressed, at 6:30 AM I am struck by the simple and direct urge to call him and say, "Are you really going to let me drive all the way to Resort Town and back by myself?" He said that he was upstairs in bed and that he would go downstairs and call me back. Twenty minutes later I look out of my window and see him dressed and helping my friend take her suitcase out of the cottage and down towards my car. He was fully dressed. By the time I came out of my apartment, he was sitting behind the wheel of my car. In surprise I said, "Are you going?" and he said, "Yes." I said, "I can drive." He said, "No, I'll drive." He really didn't look like a happy camper. Neither did my friend.

Later, Mr. told me that she looked really angry when he came to take her bags and found out that he was going to go to the airport with us. Of course, on the way home Mr. and I reconciled our differences, discussed how important the relationship was to each of us and vowed to do a better job of figuring out how we can make it work despite the inherent and seemingly insurmountable difficulties. So that, dear Another Friend, is the story of the visiting friend (now Former Friend) who backed the wrong horse.

TONI M. FORSYTH

P.S.: Interestingly enough, Former Friend just may have "weaponized" Mrs. Mr. said something yesterday about Mrs. putting her "claws" into him. He's never said anything like that before. In trying to get him to straighten up and be a "proper" husband to her, or back away from accompanying me to perform some house building related task, she may be encouraging a "fight or flight" response in him instead. He's used to passivity from her. He's used to a life where he determines when he comes and goes benevolently taking into account her needs and priorities at any given time. Remember, he spent his life as a consultant, as an employee of the British Foreign and Commonwealth Office. He's used to picking up and going about his business when required to do so with only a nod and on a you-do-not-need-to-know explanation to his spouse.

Now, with this newly developed sense of personal agency, she's exhibiting a certain degree of assertiveness, perhaps even a certain amount of aggressiveness—certainly towards me in regards to the medical procedure that he underwent and that she insisted I keep away from and again when she essentially told me to piss off when I asked her to sit in an area adjacent to the main group during a portion of the math and science event because she wasn't an active participant. "Lookie Lous" are not conducive to building group cohesion during a team building process. I wonder what will be the end result of her exercising her "rights" as his wife by telling him in which house-related activities of mine he can participate and which he cannot. I wonder if he will become more passive aggressive towards her. Or maybe just more aggressive and more frequent in his "talking roughly" to her which he has done anyway from time to time in the past. Or maybe he'll just dump me. We'll see.

It all just makes you want to go Hmmmmmm.

—Me

Shiva the Destroyer: A Final Analysis

I just got through talking to the One Person that I thought could be a friend here on Paradise Island, and it turns out that although she says she isn't taking sides with regards to Mrs. and Me, it is clear to me that she has. (But it was never supposed to be about "sides!" How did it get to be about sides? People were just supposed to go about their business as they always had. What the hell?!) I tried to tell One Person about Former Friend's bad-mouthing Mr. to both Mrs. and myself and it ended up with her not believing that Former Friend would do such a thing, and Mrs. is such a lovely person that she doesn't want to hear anything bad about her. (I never said anything about Mrs. not being a lovely person! Everybody thinks that she's a lovely person!) And I said that I'm not telling her anything bad about Mrs. just that Former Friend's interference and putting words in Mrs.' mouth in order to issue this or that directive to Mr. or respond to him in this or that particular way has interfered with a long established marital relationship dynamic and was causing a strain in the marriage that wasn't there before. Then One Person said she didn't want to hear anything bad about Former Friend because she was such a lovely person and she wasn't here to defend herself. At that point I gave up.

The rocks may have been precariously stacked on top of one another but at least they were balanced and had held their own. Now they were being dislodged one by one because somebody had come along who knew nothing of the construction process, didn't like the way the rocks looked as they were, as they had been carefully piled on top of one another over the years, and thought that she could come up with a better arrangement.

Unfortunately, the center could not hold the new and supposedly improved configuration and all hell was about to break loose.

What to do, what to do. I called "Old Friend" long distance, one that knew both Former Friend and myself. A male. I had a great conversation for over an hour. True to form, Former Friend had already disgorged some grossly distorted misinformation about me to our mutual friend that I had to correct. Why does everyone keep telling me that she means well and that she's really my friend? With friends like these, who needs enemies? I don't believe in allowing people to get away with being stupid. If there's one thing that drives me up the wall and that I cannot abide, it's stupid.

> To: Me
> From: Another Friend
> Sent: Thursday, July 24th, 6:23 AM
> Subject: Former Friend
>
> *I can't sleep. So I'm looking at email.*
>
> *I am sorry things went awry with your friend, whom you have known for a long time. She should have never taken sides, but should have made the attempt to stay neutral. I know you are in a very difficult situation, having been there myself, but I never met my paramour's wife. Maybe that made things easier, and they were never easy. I finally got out of the relationship as I decided it was going nowhere. This whole thing, Mr., his wife and your friend have sure put your life into turmoil, which you don't need with your health issues and your house.*
>
> *I don't have much else to say, except you have to work thru this in your own way and I am sorry about what happened between you and your friend. Think I will try to go back to sleep. Will write more when I have time and have more thoughts on your situation.*
>
> *—Another Friend*
> Sent from my Verizon Wireless 4G LTE DROID

To: *Another Friend*
From: *Me*
Sent: *Thursday, July 24th, 7:25 AM*
Subject: *Re: Former Friend*

At least I got a lot of stuff to write in my journal out of the experience.

—Me

To: *Another Friend*
From: *Me*
Date: *Friday, July 24th, 8:32 AM*
Subject: *My Friend*

Dear Another Friend:

Just had a long discussion on the phone with Former Friend who created such havoc last week. She said that she had seen my level of anxiety exponentially increasing during the week she was here and truly believed that what she was saying and doing would help. I told her that by repeating things to Mrs. that I had disclosed ostensibly in confidence and by advocating a particular course of action the wife should take in order to "keep her man in line" (my characterization but I believe an accurate one), her plan to remedy the situation could actually backfire because it could destabilize a relationship dynamic that had evolved over the course of half a century.

I owned up to my responsibility in the unfortunate outcome because while she was here I did exhibit a great deal of anxiety and no doubt came across as seeming to be in need of rescue. So she attempted a rescue that in actuality had, on a number of levels, the effect of making things a hell of a lot worse. For example, she apparently told Mrs. that I was too dependent on Mr. and that I needed to do things on my own in order to learn how to stand on my own two feet. I explained to her that it was precisely the folly of attempting to do things by standing on my own two feet in this highly dysfunctional, patriarchal, sexist, country that was in fact the proximate cause of the stress that led to my heart malfunction. Her advice was actually putting my very life at risk. I absolutely needed Mr.'s help with certain things otherwise I was clearly done for in more ways than one.

Anyway, all of this has certainly provided enough written material to help fill the pages of the novel that I have been writing about being a female retiree/returnee in this hell-hole of a jungle paradise.

Thanks for listening/reading and lending a psychological ear.

—Me

To: *Me*
From: *Another Friend*
Date: *Friday, July 24, 9:26 AM*
Subject: *Your Friend*

Maybe you should tell your friend that you didn't invite her to visit you to take sides especially against you. A proper friend would have tried to stay neutral, which apparently she did not (try, that is)...
Sent from my Verizon Wireless 4G LTE DROID

To: *Another Friend*
From: *Me*
Date: *Friday, July 24, 11:22 AM*
Subject: *Friend v Acquaintance*

Thanks for the comments. Just one of the little interesting things that can happen as one travels along life's highway. Too many potholes. Especially here on Paradise Island.

—Me

The Circle of Frendz

So friendships are important. Most people—not everyone, but most people—have a circle of human beings with whom they like to spend time, to socialize. I can only take so much of that—mostly because it's the same people, showing up at the same houses, saying the same things.

> *I actually got up and made a low-key retreat from a small gathering last week at the home of a friend while awaiting the serving of lunch in order to go outside and sit in my air conditioned car because I was listening to three people go on and on and on about the weather and how hot it was and how no one could remember the last time it was this hot and the plants were really suffering and how expensive it was to run the air conditioning and at certain times of the day there was a bit of a breeze to help cool things off a bit but really it was so incredibly hot but what could you do, could I offer you a glass of something cool because it really is quite hot and when you go outside and open up the car you can really feel the heat then and even when you don't have the air running inside you can tell how hot it is outside because of the difference in temperature because it's hot inside and outside but outside is even hotter because it must be the concrete or the asphalt*

TONI M. FORSYTH

or maybe it's just that it's hotter outside because when you think about it, the sun beating down all day and then you really get only a little bit of relief in the evening and the concrete building blocks actually hold the heat in because....

How could I, in good conscience, continue to sit and listen to that? It was either leave or commit suicide and at that particular moment I chose not to commit suicide but rather to sit in the air conditioned comfort of my automobile and contemplate my next move. Fright or flight?

Flight because this is what my life had devolved into.

It is to this abyss that my life had sunk. Listening to this. Oh, my God. I chose flight. And after a few minutes, I called back to the friend's house, cited my ongoing illness, gave my apologies and farewells and drove off into the heat of the day but in air-conditioned comfort. A retreat. Not necessarily a happy retreat, but a race away from insanity.

I've been a good friend to quite a few people in my time. I can listen to what different people in the same circle tell me and not take sides in the sense of outwardly throwing my allegiance toward one person over another. I learned, somewhere along the way, that you don't go behind the backs of your friends and tell the other person's business. I also learned that you don't "tell tales." That is you don't say little snippets and tidbits of information designed to highlight some drama and usually to stir up trouble among the parties involved. Most of us went through this in high school. That's what adolescence is all about. Going through those traumas so that you don't have to go through them as an adult when the consequences are far greater. Like now.

That's why people feel comfortable telling me stuff about themselves—because they sense that they can trust me not to tell. And in this way I learn an awful lot about people and what they do and how they think and how and why they treat each other the way that they do. So the person that I thought could be a friend and with whom I shared some personal information—One Person—now turns out not to be able to be a friend because she claims doesn't want to take sides because Mrs. is such a lovely person but which actually means that the person that I thought could be a friend has indeed taken sides and I'm already on the losing side and once again sidelined without a friend.

How does one exist on a steady diet of mere acquaintances? Friendship *lite*. I've lived most of my life adhering to a philosophy of "Why bother?" choosing instead for the most part to remain relatively isolated from the company of my fellow human beings because it seemed that for the most part they tended to disappoint when it came to personal integrity. Self-righteous much?

So, two friends gone within the space of a week. One, a new friend, who really never had enough time on task to even be called a friend, and although having passed the preliminary interview stage ended up flunking out during the early probationary period because she didn't understand the simple concept that one can indeed listen to all sides without taking sides. And the second friend, an old friend, ended up being terminated from the job of being a friend because she violated just about all of the most basic and sacred tenets of friendship: She carried tales between friends from one to another; she attempted to manipulate and orchestrate people's lives according to the way that she thought they should be living them. She "helicoptored" her way into a tenuous dynamic between a husband and wife, leaving an intimate relationship of longstanding duration in upheaval, brewing and simmering, leaving turmoil in her wake believing, I can only guess, that she would be able to continue her unsolicited intervention by issuing directives and monitoring the progress of her handiwork via e-mail with Mrs. from now until when? Eternity? Or at least until death doth part us all? Hers was an *RSVP* to an invitation never issued in the first place.

Sometimes it is prudent to make a happy retreat from the company of other people. Sometimes casual as well as formal interactions require too much effort, too much "grin-and-bear-it," too much taking of tea and talking of thee and me to make them worthwhile. Even the superficial, while seemingly innocuous, can end up causing as much of a strain as the more complex. There are a couple of events coming up in a few days to which I have been invited that I can either choose not to attend or use as opportunities to search the crowd for signs of intelligent life such as I recently spotted in an attorney with whom I consulted this week regarding a potential catastrophe with the ongoing nightmare that is my house. We'll see.

Casa Mia

*H*ow much about my house have I actually explained already? Have I discussed the five different contractors, the structural engineer, the two, strike that three quantity surveyors, the draughtsman, the four watchmen, the various masons, plumbers, electricians and multitude of day labourers? How about the water delivery truck owners, the two premix concrete operators, the two bulldozer operators, the sand and gravel deliverymen the cement distributors and lumberyard owners? Have I mentioned all of them before? Have I left anybody out? Have I shared that I almost lost the house to a foreclosure auction by the bank that refused to give me any details about the arrears that they claimed I owed with no explanation of the penalties and fees and fines that they said I had accumulated? ("Accountability? We don't need no stinkin' accountability!" I swear.) Did I talk about the lawyer who strung me along for the crucial two weeks prior to the scheduled forced sale until three days before the ill-fated event (which I was told by the bank manager was a done deal) when he said he really could give me no advice, and that all the things he had talked about possibly doing in the end he couldn't really do? How I found another lawyer two days before doomsday who told me to go to the main branch of the bank in Capital City 1½ hours drive away and show them a whole heap of cash, as much as I could possibly put together by fair means or foul? And how I asked Mr. to accompany me and he did, and I poured a whole heap of cash out of a black plastic bag onto the table and the two bank representatives' eyes lit up like neon lights

TONI M. FORSYTH

and they said sure, we'll pull the house from the auction block? And how I still don't know how the arrears were calculated or the fines or the fees or the penalties? That's what it means to live in a corrupt banana republic. "Banking regulations? We don't need no stinkin' banking regulations. We make them up as we go and anything goes!"

To: Another Friend
From: Me
Date: Friday, July 25, 9:14 AM
Subject: Friend v Acquaintance

Hi Another Friend:

There are different kinds of friends. Some will pick up the kids after school when you are in a bind and some will pick up the newspaper from the driveway if you forget to put a vacation hold on your delivery service. Different levels of effort involved. One is a good buddy, the other is a good neighbor.

So, I followed up my phone call to my Former Friend with an e-mail about how a good emotional support friend is above all else a good listener.

Sometimes a friend just needs to talk, to vent; when that happens, the other is there to listen. I used the analogy of the pressure cooker with a safety valve that occasionally needs to let off steam. One never wants to go poking around inside the volatile internal process bubbling along because what one will end up with if one does is a god-awful mess on the walls, ceiling and floor and on anybody who happens to be in the way.

My own philosophy of how to be a good emotional friend involves the dictum that for the most part, action is neither required nor desirable unless bodily harm is imminent. In fact, a prime directive of non-interference is to be held sacrosanct. Talk and listen, that's it. Questions are fine and if they are the right ones can be quite useful.

Friends differ from acquaintances in that one trusts a friend not to reveal to others that which has been shared in private. (Although, if it comes right down to it, one must always keep squarely in mind that one should never say anything to anybody that he or she doesn't want printed on the front page of the daily newspaper.)

Not so an acquaintance. One chooses one's friends very carefully based on the belief that one thinks one has seen in the other person similar values and behaviours, and there exists a high degree of mutual respect between the two such that harsh judgments are not likely to be passed.

With this definition in mind, what say you?

—Me

To: Me
From: Another Friend
Date: Friday, July 25, 7:27 PM
Subject: Re: Friend v Acquaintance

Before freud came along, people had no choice but to vent to each other. nowadays with therapists one can vent to them, especially with the health plan coverage at the HMO where I'm a physician. I guess we all have stressful lives and life is often difficult, more so for some people than others. I have been going to therapists off and on for many years, as I feel pretty stressed from time to time. I know whatever I say there will not go beyond that room. one can hope that of friends, but there is no guarantee that what you say will not be repeated.

A good friend is someone who can listen as you said, and NOT BE JUDGMENTAL. that is what your friend was doing. she was only there temporarily, she is not part of your family, so in my opinion, it would have been best had she stayed out of it as much as possible (but we are only human in that regard).

When it comes to venting to friends, and I do that too, as well as the therapist thing, I feel it is important to share the wealth. try to spread it around to different people plus different people are interested in different aspects of your life, often relating your experiences to their own lives. that's why, for instance, my HMO has grief group therapy for people suffering similar kind of pain. it's a lot easier to empathize with someone who is going thru what you are, like divorce, for instance.

I think you were a very good friend when I was going thru my divorce. you did a lot of listening as I recall and I was seeing a therapist then. I was looking for all the help I could get. Some people don't want to hear it, so better to look for someone else who is willing to listen. your brother was also a help to me at that time, maybe, its a male thing, but not only did he listen, he often would say what he thought I should do about whatever problem it was. so I would listen and try to make up my own mind what to do. or sometimes I would talk to someone else about the same problem, sort of poll the delegation as it were. but I think men often say something: "I am telling you, this is what you need to do, so you better do it because I know best, or something like that."

My dad used to annoy me because I would tell him a problem I had and he would not listen, would tell me what to do and then if I didn't do what he said, he would get disgusted and say: "I don't want to hear about that anymore!" well, that was him, and I don't think I would look for that response in a friend. that is, the price of listening to your problem, being, to unquestioningly take his, my dad's, advice. the penalty being: no further advice on that subject would be given in the future. period!

I have a friend now. I do most of the listening. I think I mentioned him to you before. we worked together at the HMO and became friends. he hated the HMO and really wanted to be on his own. so he moved to louisiana and started his own business (medical legal stuff connected with job injuries). in a way he sort of shot himself in the foot.

He had a pretty good life in Flagstaff. he didn't work that hard at the HMO, had friends, played tennis, was in a tennis club. when he moved to louisiana, he lost everything but his work. he literally is working 16 hours a day. he has no life outside of work, not sure exactly why, maybe Baton Rouge is a hard place to break into. so he talks to me, and talks and talks. and runs things by me, even little things. I guess in a way I feel I am paying it forward, for all the listening people did for me over the years. and I guess in a way I feel flattered to be his confidant as I have always liked him a lot. I think in a way he made a mistake moving to LA and now he feels trapped with the huge amt of $$ he makes there in a more lucrative place for him vs. his homesickness, which he didn't realize he had, for Arizona. but anyway, I think I am being a good friend.

So these are some thoughts on my part about friends.

—Another Friend

To: *Another Friend*
From: *Me*
Date: *Tuesday, July 29, 6:59 PM*
Subject: *Re: Friend v Acquaintance*

Hi Another Friend:

Thanks for your thoughtful response on friends and the various kinds of friendships that cross our paths over the course of a lifetime. You've certainly been a friend to me during the various incarnations of our almost 50 (!) year friendship, and from your descriptions of what you bring to the table of your other friendships, you are quite commodious in your adaptations to the varying needs of others as circumstances dictate.

You mention spreading "the wealth." I think it would be fortunate indeed to have come across enough people to warrant a "spreading" with whom one would want to share any of the personal details of one's life. I can't imagine finding people who could really be totally judgment free. Even if you consider as benign an example as thinking why would anyone want to eat a Mounds bar when for the same price you could buy an Almond Joy and get the extra added benefit of the nutritious almond? There is even a judgment there that could perhaps unhinge the most sensitive of those among us. Just kidding!

I'm now engaged in contemplating the fact that there are so many people out there who are absolutists or "black and white" thinkers. These are folks who have very rigid standards for behavior and/ or being-in-the-world (in a philosophical sense). I suppose it must bring a great deal of comfort to have clear cut, proscribed recipes for how to respond in any given situation or how to live one's life no matter what complications come one's way, but how can they ever be a good friend if they can't appreciate the nuances inherent in individual lives and respond accordingly; that is, the recipe has to be altered to fit the altitude at which the meal is being prepared. Or the temperature changed for the meal that is being cooked. Or allow for a different baking time when using the glass baking dish as opposed to the metal pan.

I suppose that since it may very well be that since the majority of people do indeed live black and white lives, that kind of thinking serves them quite well. But for those of us whose lives do not readily tend toward the dichotomous, the friendship that those folks offer can in the end only be superficial, not deep. Acquaintance-like. But then perhaps that is better than nothing. Sometimes.

—Me

To: Me
From: Another Friend
Date: Tuesday, July 30, 4:55 PM
Subject: Re: Friend v Acquaintance

Yes, I have noticed the black and white thing, that some people do not think in shades of gray (no allusion to the book by a similar name). I like to think that having grown up as an army brat and lived many different places before coming to the REAL Holy Land, Arizona, that I observed and learned that there are many ways to live in this world, all with varying degrees of success, but almost all having some merit.

People have survived all over the world with different ways of life and unless they are unusually cruel, as some of the stuff in the Middle East, honor killings and such, we should all try and accept these differences. In my life, I have been to over 30 countries and all 50 states, and every trip I have made is an education especially he one I just finished, to Israel and Jordan.

Yes, the "my way or the highway" mentality has always bugged me.

—Another Friend

July 27th

*M*r. and Mrs. and I along with a few others were all invited to dine at the home of friends located about a 10-15 minutes drive out of Tourist Town, about a 25 minutes drive from My Happy Retreat. It ended up with Mr., certainly unbeknownst to him, being a prop in a piece of performance art. A little theater piece staged by Mrs. for the benefit of mutual friends gathered together for Sunday afternoon brunch at a lovely hillside home overlooking an azure blue sea framed by a white sand cove on a scorching hot day.

She made of him what in the local parlance is known as a "poppy show" (probably a variation of "puppet" show). She coordinated their wardrobes so that they were both dressed in all-white cotton muslin—she in a kind of Carmen Miranda-like ruffled knee length skirt and he in a loose fitting pull-over shirt and draw string pants reminiscent of Harry Belafonte singing "Day-O." Costumes each, conceived no doubt to eternalize in the minds of our friends that they are indeed a couple, a paired and boxed set fixed and immutable in the firmament of celestial constellations. But in the immortal words of Groucho Marx, "A couple of what?"

She has taken to power walks, abs exercises and wears mud masks to forestall the ravages of time. But when people see her, their comment invariably is, "She looks good for her age." Her age is what it is. The makeup is artfully applied (remember, she was in the theater). She recently got a shorter more youthful haircut, the multi-colored mix of gray hair is now closer to blonde, but she is still an elderly woman pushing 80. The too youthful outfits along with the woefully out-of-date dresses and skirts are some of the tell tale signs that she is either trying too hard or not trying hard enough. But to drag her husband into her deception had an effect on me for which I was not prepared.

I arrived an hour late to the gathering, having suffered from the effects of too much sun after having spent about 20 minutes earlier that morning washing my car because it was impossibly filthy. I was off center, finding it a little difficult to stand without swaying so I decided to lie down for a bit before I finished getting dressed. When I arrived at the home of my friends, I actually found walking from the car and down the stairs into their house just a little difficult as well. The hostess held my arm and guided me to a chair in the living room, sat me down and handed me a glass of water to drink before I made the rest of the trek out to the front verandah where the rest of the guests were seated.

Mrs. was definitely not pleased to see me. She grew quiet, whereas before I had heard her voice as part of the general conversation. My outfit was a bright red silk with a deep maroon border and bright yellow, lime and orange accents. It stood out in contrast to the all white outfits worn by Mr. and Mrs. My hostess pulled up a chair for me to sit in. It was right next to Mr. He greeted me by turning and incorporating me into the ongoing conversation. It was then that I noticed what he was wearing and what she was wearing. It registered slowly that they were meant to be matching outfits. I felt a kind of creeping, unpleasant sensation of which I was only just barely aware. An overly dramatic response I know and really only perceptible to me on a subconscious level, but it was still there. The luncheon continued over the course of about three hours. Food served, drinks poured, conversation engaged, we sat at different tables Mr. and Mrs. at one and I at another.

When it came time to depart, Mr. and Mrs. were the first to leave. He kissed each of the women in turn on the cheek and when he came to me. I backed away. Totally unplanned. I had no idea why I was doing it, but I didn't want him to touch me. But the fact is I was creeped out. She had emasculated him. He was no longer Bwana. He was an actor in a Punch and Judy show. It was the *Comedia d'ell Arte* and he was Harlequin in summer garb, the usual multitude of colors now transformed into all white. It was her having dominion over him. It dated him. It aged him. It made him the equivalent of the aging Jewish retiree in South Beach minus the gold chains and diamond pinky ring. The matching outfits idea was something my sister would have come up with straight out of the 1950's. I didn't want him to touch me. I didn't know who that man was.

When I got home I became afraid. I got really scared. It was if some existential nightmare had been set in motion and the person I now loved more than anyone in the world, literally my saviour, had been annihilated. The dignified land owner, the settler of disputes, the superior mind, the leader of men had been swept from the face of the earth and an inferior entity now held sway over the shell of the man I had held in my arms and who had held me in his so many times when I was so ill and actually dying and made me feel safe and secure. I told you this could seem overly dramatic, but it is honest-to-God how I felt about what I saw, and how I still feel the day after and the day after that. Things would continue to change.

The atmosphere has changed. She's still keeps to herself inside the house most of the time, but the matching outfits were a clear declaration of territorial rights and a "Private Property/No Trespassing" sign. I think there's been a formal declaration of war. Official Dispatch received.

Next

He really wants me to finish my house. How many years has it been now? Is it for him or for me? He needs a "project." I need a monument to my isolation and loneliness like I need a hole in my head (or more atrial fibrillation in my heart).

August 9th

*O*cean Beach Restaurant and Bar. Mai Tai's and a moonlit night overlooking the cove with the colored lights at play below. How could two people not be swept up in the moment there and then?

When will their son's house be sold and the one with the in-law apartment purchased so Mrs. and ostensibly Mr. can escape to a happier place and perhaps in her own mind a happier time when she was younger and presumably happier because of the many distractions and delights that a First World country and a cosmopolitan city afforded? When will Mrs. let go of the anger that has built up inside of her about the reality of her aging, the face in the mirror no longer reflecting the one she had relied upon so much in the past? When will she stop seeing me as the one who has now made her life a "living hell" as she so often characterized the process of change from merely mature to decidedly elderly woman? I'm beginning to wonder if Mrs. no longer has that cosmopolitan destination on her list of places to be. Thank you so much Former Friend and One Person. I had thought the cosmopolitan life was what Mrs. had wanted. At one time it had been. At this moment, perhaps not so much? Things had changed.

TONI M. FORSYTH

August 10th

Morning: Coffee on the patio under the almond tree; philosophical discussion. Mrs. was asked to join but declined. I could feel that Mr. and I were laughing and talking too much for our own good. I offer to go with him for his blood tests on Monday morning.

Late Afternoon: No, he's going with Mrs. for the blood tests. Found out. I called him. As usual. Change of plans. Honestly? Repeatedly. Often enough that it sends me up the wall. I have no say. I have no control. Lucky I found out the afternoon before and not the morning of. Things have definitely changed. She's taking charge, taking control. Taking names and kicking ass. Was it all Former Friend and One Person or was some other force on the move?

I started out as a visitor to the asylum, and now I've become one of the inmates. I've got to get the hell out of here.

August 11th

*H*e called and said he wanted to meet me in my car. He told me that Mrs. had jumped up from her chair on the opposite side of the room the night before and plunked her self down beside Mr. in order to listen in on our phone conversation! I was shocked. I could not believe a grown woman would do that. She has lost her sense of self-respect and dignity. He told her as much. He said that he told her he had never looked in her handbag nor gone through her mail and for her to so ostentatiously eavesdrop on a private conversation that he was having with me was tantamount to that kind of behaviour. She apologized an hour later. Mr. says she also asked him if he loved me. He says he told her that he would not answer such a question and that the question was irrelevant. (But what about the answer?) She was his wife and he was loyal to her.

What did she make of that?

P.S.: Shiva the Destroyer (Former Friend) used all the things that I told her (supposedly in confidence) that Mrs. was doing or not doing with regards to Mr. as talking points on what Mrs. should or should not be doing in order to be a better wife to him! My distraught recitation was converted into a laundry list of things to do in order to win back her man! Shiva the Trojan Horse. Mixed metaphors. Or symbols. Or literary allusions. But I know you get my drift. Oh, the perfidy! Oh, the betrayal! Good thing I'm keeping a record. If I weren't, I'd tell myself to do just that. Write a book. Because who would believe it? I certainly would not have believed that I could have dug myself in so deep.

TONI M. FORSYTH

He just called from Capital City (unbeknownst to me that he was even going)—an unplanned trip with Mrs. because, so he said, his doctor asked him for the results of some lab tests that he had done. Breaking News! It turns out that the real reason that they went was because Mrs. wanted to get herself checked out! She's been having rapid heartbeat and shortness of breath. (Sound familiar?) Couldn't she at least be original with her symptoms? I guess whatever works.

Mental Notes to Mr.:

First: Thank you for calling to let me know what is going on, where you were today. Your call meant more than you know.

Second: What can I do with the terrible feeling of impotence that I am experiencing right now when somebody I love, the somebody I love, is in my opinion, having his health seriously jeopardized (still with the eyes, next up—prostate) and I am utterly helpless to do anything about it? You know how you would feel if our roles were reversed. Your outward reaction would be extreme—visibly far worse than mine is right now because I turn my emotions inward. My outward reactions—as effusive as you think they are—are nothing compared to what is going on inside of me. Hence, the arrhythmia. My heart is literally beating wildly out of control over what is happening to you.

For utterly selfish, extraordinarily self-centered, self-aggrandizing and wholly unnecessary reasons Mrs. is once again putting your health at risk by having you make the drive into Capital City in the un-air conditioned jalopy of a vehicle that you use to haul produce to the market. You are reduced to making phone calls in secret. You have allowed yourself to surrender to pique, to be the servant of caprice. There is no honor in that.

I will **make a list** of the things that need to be done throughout your house to help your ongoing problems with allergies but particularly what to do to put an end to your constant attacks of rhinitis. I myself suffer from allergic reactions to my environment, and my poor sister suffered her whole life as well. In short, based *on a lifetime of my personal experiences as well as my research on the topic, please believe me when I say that I may have more practical knowledge than even your doctor as to what needs to be done to alleviate your suffering sinuses. If you doubt me and need me to provide citations as references for the interventions and remedies that I suggest, I will do so.*

At what price loyalty? Martyrdom? At least speak up on your own behalf and act in your own best interests when the opportunities present themselves. You could have borrowed my car. I'm not so selfish as to wish you to make the drive into the city in this unbearable world-wide Climate Change heat if, and only if, I'm in the car. It is always at your disposal with or without me. You do not have to swallow the whole cup of hemlock that Mrs. insists you drink! "Look to the heavens from whence cometh thy help."

I offer what I can, but I remain at once stunned and appalled and feel so very helpless.

TONI M. FORSYTH

August 15th

To: Another Friend
From: Me
Date: Friday, August 15, 9:14 AM
Subject: The Latest

Are you still in the continental U.S. or somewhere more exotic? I wanted to fill you in on the latest crisis here at Happy Retreat.

Mrs. went in for a whole battery of tests over the course of this week because her blood pressure has been periodically elevated and she was afraid she was going to have a stroke (my analysis from the information I've been given by Mr.). Apparently she had a whole battery of tests—even one where she was hooked up all over to electrodes and was monitored for 24 hours. Seems excessive, but so I've been told.

Apparently it's now come out that it's all because of my relationship with Mr. or Mr.'s relationship with me (not sure which or both). More likely the fantasy of the extent to which Mr. and I are intending to obliterate her world as she knows as described to her in great, embellished detail by One Person. In any event, whenever he's with me for an extended period of time the panic kicks in and sends her vitals over the edge. Otherwise her health is fine.

According to Mr., she's been told to get a grip otherwise she'll blow a gasket and die.

He has a doctor's appointment today in the city (slightly enlarged prostate with symptoms he could no longer ignore), and I was supposed to go along so I could see my doctor as well for a quick visit because I've been experiencing shortness of breath and on multiple occasions have felt as if I was going to pass out (cold and clammy sweats, unable to stand, etc.), but she told Mr. that if he went with me, he'd come back to find her dead—presumably from a stroke. So I wasn't allowed go. She would go instead.

But I have an appointment scheduled for Monday morning with my doctor, and if she won't let me go, then I'll be the one he'll find dead. All of this courtesy of my so-called friend, Former Friend, who visited last month and took it upon herself to relate to Mrs. information that I had shared with her in confidence. And also One Person friend. Because of that interference, Mrs. has become unglued and I may die. The wages of sin, etc.

So that's the latest in a nutshell. Stay tuned for the next installment in "As the Stomach Churns." Barf!

—Me

*O*f course, I myself am already coming unglued. Have been for quite a while now. I believe that all of my recent near-fainting spells, out-of-breath episodes and elevated heart rate are the result of a constant state of unrelenting anxiety and the reoccurrence of depression. Yes, I do have on-going thoughts of regaining some control over my life by holding in my hands a bottle of pills, the means by which I can end it.

The recent death of Robin Williams has not helped. His suicide was not all that surprising—I had seen a television interview with him not too long ago by Jon Stewart on *The Daily Show*, and it was clear the man had demons that needed to be exorcised. His thrashing and flailing about in some of his comic routines were an indication of the extent to which he was willing to go in a desperate attempt to escape. It's just that one suicide—especially a very public one—makes it easier for the next one to occur. I guess it's the way by which the universe grants permission to provide a readily available means of relieving oneself of the unbearable pain of dealing with the never-ending Armageddon being fought inside one's head.

So Mr. just called me from his doctor's office. Mrs. wants me to apologize for embarrassing her at the math and science event last month. Pardon me while I pick myself up from the floor after falling off my chair in utter amazement. Me apologize to her! I can't wait for this little drama to play itself out. Tentatively scheduled for tomorrow. Let's see what happens.

TONI M. FORSYTH

Other Dramatis Personae: The Greek Chorus

The Circle of Frendz: Bernie and Pepper, Gerald and Jeri, Ryan and Sharlene—the recipients of bits and pieces of information regarding crimes real and imagined against the wronged wife funneled through the repackaged, retelling of the tale by Pepper (aka One Person) and the distorted mental gymnastics (courtesy of the clinically depressed mind) of Mrs.—with at least two of the six proclaiming moral superiority and the right to cast the first, second and third stones. My account of the events that transpired is dead on. I know because I was there. I saw them happen. Mrs. had withdrawn from the stage for the better part of a year and nursed her existential succubus until she could attach a face to it, and now she's using emotional blackmail and intimidation to try to regain control of her life. Does anybody have the right to do that? Righteous indignation speaks out in my mind: "I don't care how many years in the trenches she has spent or how many titles of ownership she can produce." There are others who would say those are the very reasons that give her license. You play, you pay. The Greek Chorus speaks, the audience listens.

The Circle of Frendz: Numbers one and two. Bernie is much like the townsperson who, when the Nazis marched in, bolted his doors and closed his windows, drew his curtains and shuttered his shop and said to his frau, "Don't get involved! Don't listen. Close your ears. It has nothing to do with us." Pepper, his wife, did not listen to her husband but chose to get involved, to make herself important by betraying her neighbor and friend, by telling what she knew and repackaging what she had learned to fit in with her own life story as well as with what she now determined must certainly be a national *cause célèbre*. She thought she was seeing a slow-motion replay of her own past taking place before her very eyes in the fate that was surely befalling the woman who had now accepted fantasy as reality, who was looking for ammunition to support her delusions about a world she could no longer control and a reality she could no longer forestall. Bernie had bought into the fantasy, but he thought he could still keep his distance from the real world of consequences. But when the time came, just like Camus' schoolteacher, he couldn't not end up being involved. He could not escape; he could not simply retreat behind his four walls pretending what was taking place inside and out was none of his business. In the end, everyone will be held accountable for their presence in the arena, for both their action and inaction.

> *"The mirror is no longer my friend. Who do I blame? Who is at fault? Where do I point the finger? Who is responsible for the terrible calamity that is befalling me and the existence that I had so carefully constructed, so painstakingly nurtured over the course of a lifetime? Aha! I've spotted the enemy in my midst. I see her now. As plain as day. Off with her head!"*

In real life, the Nazi officer who came into that German town so very long ago (or maybe not so very long ago after all) wasn't even looking to roust the Jews who had lived there for generations. It was a handful of townspeople who thought that they could curry favour with the higher ups in the advancing army by pointing out the scapegoats that led the assault. They are the ones who set out to round up their terrified Jewish neighbours, their friends, the people with whom they had gone to school and with whom their children had gone to school and drive them into the barn with pitchforks and shovels as weapons, and lock the barn doors and set it on fire and when the terrified people tried to run free shoot them or bludgeon them to death. Their German (but weren't they all Germans by birth?) friends and acquaintances and neighbours, and did I say friends?

TONI M. FORSYTH

In the story by Camus, the guest is both protected from harm and delivered up to his fate. We can try to shirk our duty to honour the Thou, but in fact we cannot remain to one side, we cannot close our eyes, we cannot not get involved. We cannot escape our call to account: We are destined to be held accountable for that which we do and that which we do not do. And we are destined to grow older—by each second, each minute, each hour, each day—and to live with the consequences of our actions for each of those intervals that remains.

The Circle of Frendz: Numbers three and four. Gerald the jealous, Gerald the insecure. Gerald who eagerly anticipates any opportunity to feel superior to Mr., and because Mrs. is such a "lovely person" and he "loves" her, cares about her happiness and her well being, and could see she's been upset of late, he is compelled to speak up, to tell what he thinks he knows, what he thinks he has seen. And yet his own wife cowers when he browbeats her on the few occasions when she voices an opinion contrary to his own. And he beat his sons when they were growing up. An unsolicited admission. An "anger management" problem he says. Something he knows he needs to work on. At this late date? Never too late? Yet he wants to stage an intervention with Mr. as the target held on behalf of Mrs. to try and set Mr. straight. Pull a few of Mr.'s close male friends together, enlist the aid even of those who live overseas with a few phone calls (Can you believe it?) to point out the error of Mr.'s ways, to point out the hurt that he has inflicted on his loving wife. But no one has ever talked to Mr. No one has heard his take. His affirmation or his denial. No one questions Pepper's retelling of the tale. Not one.

The mote in one's eye. He who is without sin, *et cetera, et cetera.*

Yet it is those well-meaning friends with their tales told out of school who added unnecessary fuel to the smoldering embers of the self stoked fire and caused the conflagration to ignite manifesting itself first as an ulcer and now perhaps as a more serious ailment in Mrs. It is they who took bits and pieces of the truth in order to concoct a tasty repast upon which to dine.

The Circle of Frendz: Numbers five and six. Ryan and Sharlene, salt of the earth types. Not the kind to instigate trouble types. Kind and fair-minded types. And also two people who themselves have suffered life threatening illnesses over the course of the last year. These are the slow-and-steady-wins-the-race types. Neutralizing influence types.

These are the members of Mr.'s inner circle who one by one offered their opinions regarding the current state of affairs and their commentary on the impact that events real and imagined had had upon the life of Mrs. And still no one asks how Mr. feels, his account of the facts; no one asks Mr.'s opinion about anything until recently, when confronted one afternoon by Mrs. and Bernie and Pepper over cups of tea, he expressed his opinion regarding me that perhaps...

> *"That is not what [she] meant at all:*
> *That is not it at all."*

And of course, no one wants to hear from me directly. The reality of me is now wholly irrelevant to the situation as it now stands. No one wants to jeopardize the grand narrative of their own design. Mrs. believes her own interpretation of events to be a factual account, locked as she is in a world of her own making, and none of the members of the Circle of Frendz has any intention of making any inquiries of me, relying solely, perhaps, on Pepper's admonition to me to leave town. To get out. To go away. To go back where I came from (Yes, that's what she told me! Can you imagine?) because I am the "Other Woman."

August 18th

I'm trying to wrap this up. I am continuing to experience some of the symptoms that landed me in the hospital a year ago, so I'm running out of steam. I'm definitely in the middle of something: shortness of breath, the sensation of a furnace heating up inside me during the night, general weakness, continued weight loss. Today, Mrs. wouldn't allow(!) Mr. to drive me to the city to see my doctor. Mrs. and I had a **BIG** talk on the patio yesterday morning at the end of which she agreed to let him drive me but then, later on in the afternoon, she changed her mind (just as I very much suspected she would). She also told me she believes with unwavering certainty that I deliberately set out to embarrass her at the math and science event by not letting her sit at a table with the participants despite my well-reasoned and experienced-based rationale for requesting that she not do so. I did this, she believes, in retribution for the fact that she told me to leave the pre-op room before the doctor arrived for Mr.'s medical procedure. She also told Mr. that she was hurt by the fact that I did not throw my arms around her and greet her warmly on the morning of her return from her second trip to the U.K. when I was quite literally dying from congestive heart failure. After struggling to dress, pack and drag my body out of my apartment to get to the airport on time, I spotted her and asked desperately, frantically for the whereabouts of the car that was to drive me to the airport, to get me to the emergency room in Miami, still hours away, in order to save my life. But she truly believes I needed to be focused on her return to My Happy Retreat. She took my behavior as a rejection of her and as evidence that I no longer considered her a friend. That she had been cast on the waste heap, discarded in favor of the eminently more desirable Mr. So she now inexplicably says.

Tonight I had a total emotional melt down because even though I took a cold shower, sweat was pouring down my face. My heart rate shot up. I had difficulty breathing. I called Mr. He came over with Mrs. in tow and I screamed at her to get out because she was killing me and that she was a Horrible Person for not letting him take me to the doctor, and I screamed and screamed and chased her out waving my blood pressure monitor in her face, and what my absolute impulse was at that moment was to bash her over the head with it and hopefully kill her and put an end to her arbitrary control over whether I lived or died.

I did need somebody I could trust to take me to the doctor. Yes I did end up the next day letting Mr. take me to the doctor 20 minutes away in Tourist Town. That eminent physician told me that I wasn't going to die immediately because, in his estimation, the problem was just that my heart wasn't pumping enough blood to my head. Oh, that's all it was! But hold on. I soon realized that his ability to help me long term would not be forthcoming because what he said was what I really needed was to go to the hairdresser and pamper myself. Perhaps distract myself with a hobby or get some exercise by puttering around in the garden. And my hot flashes and sweats were caused by menopause. Ha ha. He would be censured in the U.S. for saying something like that to a female patient, perhaps even charged with malpractice. And he prescribed a medication that would have ended up masking the symptoms that were key to identifying the real nature of my current health problems. My U.S. cardiologist subsequently ordered a cutting edge test that would determine what was or was not causing my current symptoms.

TONI M. FORSYTH

The Proximate Cause of My Full Blown Anxiety Attack: The Inmate is Now Running the Asylum

The nightmare has begun:

There's been a takeover: the inmate is running the asylum. The Medusa has wrested the keys from the Keeper, has slammed and bolted the doors and windows tightly shut and is holding everyone hostage inside the asylum. One of the inmates/prisoners is ill and she won't let the Keeper take that person to the doctor in the City on the other side of the hill. The Evil Queen is reliving her parental abandonment and control issues and wreaking havoc on the lives of the people she has locked inside.

She is in charge now, making the rules about who goes or stays, who lives or dies. The façade is gone, the mask removed and now the Wicked Witch of the West is unveiled for all to see. The inmate in the nightmare who needs to go to the doctor is really me, and I end up going to pieces, having a total meltdown. I am no longer me. I am a madwoman; I go insane because I am no longer free, I am no longer in control of whether I live or die. I scream and flail my arms and chase the Horrible Person, the Wicked Witch, the Evil Queen away from my cell. I want to kill her, to smash her head with the monitoring device that's been attached to my body, to wipe the look of astonishment from the Wicked Witch's face. At once both excited and frightened by the commotion, the dog at the door is barking furiously, frantically, whipped up now into a canine frenzy.

Maybe the dog will tear into the Wicked Witch, into the Evil Queen's leg and she'll fall down the stairs and die. Maybe I will actually push her, trip her, kill her myself then everyone under her thrall will be free. She slowly backs away, down the stairs leaving me alone with the Keeper and the bewildered dog who herself eventually, silently slinks away taking refuge in her own little corner of solitude.

For a while, the House of Bedlam reigned supreme: hysteria ruled the night air and utter despair prevailed. But in the end, for all to see, the Evil Queen was unmasked, tried at last, and now finally convicted of crimes against humanity. The words were clear. There was no doubt. She told the Keeper in no uncertain terms, she would not allow him to take me to the doctor. She would hold sway over whether I lived or died.

As described before, at first decree there would have been no conveyance to a doctor: not the one in the City an hour and a half's drive from where we live or the one 20 minutes away in Tourist Town. Too much time together would have to be spent during the trip to the City, and I could just drive myself to the doctor nearer to home.

In the end Mr. prevailed. I was dizzy. I could pass out and have an accident. I was incapable of driving. In the end, in the office, the nurse put me in a wheelchair, wheeled me into the examining room and helped me on to the examining table. I felt dizzy sitting up, I felt dizzy lying down, I began to sob. "Please don't let me die." The doctor reassured me, "No, you're not going to die." I was not so sure. But at least not that day.

Note Bene: **Postscript: Spoiler Alert: Timeline Out-of-Sequence:** It would take another 5 weeks for me to find out that this hyperventilated meltdown was fueled by one of the heart medications that I was taking. I had continued for several weeks after the episode chronicled above on my dizzying path quite literally toward impending self-destruction since a drug-induced psychosis led me into full blown suicidal ideation. No two ways about it: I had an overwhelming urge to off myself. Utterly compelling day after day. Thank God for a post-graduate education and having grown up in a family of medical doctors and for having simply paid enough attention and read enough research studies over the years to finally figure out what the hell was going on with me and why I was tightly grasping, in daily contemplation, a bottle of sleeping pills in my hand when I went to bed each night.

I managed to figure out which med was causing the reaction and stopped taking it. Just like that the compulsion went away. I tried taking half the dosage a few days later: The urge returned. A few days after that, and after a disastrous session with a woefully inadequate psychotherapist to which Mr. was grudgingly allowed to drive me, I tried a one-quarter dosage. Same reaction. No go, so no more. I am left to wrestle with my cardiologist as to what medication to try next to keep the physical demons at bay, the psychological ones currently harnessed—at least for the present.

August 19th: Payback Time?

Is it possible that there might come a Payback Time for him? He chuckles at my mention of my wanting to jerk Mrs.' chain by showing up at a charity event at the Great House on Saturday. He marveled at the expression on her face when I showed up at a recent tea for guests visiting from England. My car was used to chauffer them—I get to make an appearance to retrieve it. His big thing has been to try and deal with her rationally—an appeal to reason. However, as anybody with half a brain but Mr. could see, her responses are not rational. They are not coming from a place of reason but a place of reaction and emotion: To me. To us. To Mr. and me. To the reality of her relationship with Mr. from the time they first met: despite the marriage, despite the children, despite the life shared over the years and across continental divides. Mrs. and I are both having emotional meltdowns, the two women in Mr.'s life. Hers is fueled by panic, mine by anxiety. Is this what happens at this stage in one's life when the stakes are so high? At least there's a pre-existing physiological component to go along with mine. Word up! One up!

So could he of the rational, reasonable mind be getting fed up, especially when she tells him that he can't drive me to see the doctor. Today, he has been as loving and tender to me as ever. In public places. It's as if he's telling her, "Here, take that!" A caress, a kiss more holding of hands and fingers intertwined. Let's see what the next few days will bring. Payback Time? We'll see.

TONI M. FORSYTH

"I can't drive the woman for whom I care so much to see her doctor? Too much time being spent together? I'll show you. We'll drive our cars separately to a rendezvous point, meet up and continue our journey in one car."

That's what we did today. Not to the city, but so that Mr. could take me to get blood samples drawn to try and get a handle on what's causing my latest symptoms.

"You can't keep us apart. We're like teenagers who have been forbidden to have anything to do with each other by our parents. Screw you, wife. I'm in love with my lover and you can't tell me not to be. Especially since I was never in love with you to begin with." (I keep coming back to that!) "Especially since you trapped me into marrying you by getting pregnant when I was just a kid. Eighteen when we first met for God's sake! Especially since my mother hated you for it. And especially since trying to deny someone access to medical treatment is just plain wicked. And besides, you've known all along for all of these years that I was never in love with you, and you chose to hang in and go along with it anyway. Do you think you're winning out now? Winning me over? Could you possibly think that this is your moment of triumph? Could you even possibly be that deluded?"

Of course this says nothing about his culpability over the years in maintaining the charade. But then again, he did his duty, upheld to the greatest extent humanly possible to his end of the deal. These are Faustian deals that people make in order to live their lives according to the social dictates of their times. It's just that sometimes the real-life human beings outlive the mores of the times during which the bargains were made. What then? Who knew so many of us would live for so long?

You made your bed, so you must lie in it. For how long? For as long as it takes.

Anyway, so I'm wondering if this is what is going through his head because he doesn't allow himself to entertain emotional responses to situations (at least that's what he says). He doesn't stress, he just adapts. And what I've just supposed to be his true feelings are, of course, just suppositional on my part. And I don't know any of this for a fact, but all of it sure sounds plausible enough to me.

Is he actually turning the knife ever so slowly, counter clockwise into the small of her back? But then again, maybe that knife is actually pointed at me.

Letter to Mr.: I am a Lost Puppy

I am a lost puppy who found its way to your doorstep. You gave the puppy a home. You nurtured it and gave it a kind of strength that it had not previously experienced even before it got sick. You became its friend, its kindred spirit without either you or the puppy realizing that that was what was taking place. Amazing.

But the puppy is sick now and has nowhere else to go. I'm not sure what will happen next because it's developing new symptoms every few days and really needs to see the really good doctors far, far away. You offered the best solution that you thought you could at the time which was to send the puppy away all on its own and tell it to lie down on somebody else's doorstep (which seemed to the puppy a very cruel thing to suggest), but how could you possibly think that would have worked out? I think if you had thought it

TONI M. FORSYTH

through, you would have realized that on your own, but I understand that you were under a great deal of pressure at the time to respond quickly.

This is one of the problems that can occur when you take in strays. You can't always just feed them and then put them back out unattended to fend for themselves. Sometimes they become too domesticated and forget how to take care of themselves or just can't because they were so bruised and so battered for so long they can never really recuperate enough to survive on their own again. That's me now. The sick puppy who has nowhere else to go.

I have decided that I am more like the dog that the master has decided he doesn't want anymore, and has locked outside and stopped feeding. The dog continues to sit at the front door waiting to be fed, expecting the master to open it up at any minute and welcome him back in, but he waits in vain. I am that dog.

The Forces of Darkness

*N*o doctors or blood tests for me until I'm well enough to drive myself or am willing to pay a local taxi man to drive me, and I must make sure that while I'm on my own, I don't faint and hit my head when I pass out and fall to the ground along the way!

The way I'm feeling now, the forces of darkness have won. Her mojo is more powerful than mine—or his. I guess that's life. But in the end, I think he could have played his hand a bit differently. I think today's the day I must go gently into that good night. I must embrace the dying of the light. *Goodnight Moon.*

August 22nd: "Off With Her Head!"

From: Me
To: Mr.
Sent: Friday, August 22, 9:43 AM
Subject: Off with Her Head!

You took me on, you drew me in at a time when I was desperate and my very life depended on someone throwing me a lifeline. To dump me now, to suggest that we'll just be around each other from time to time when circumstance dictates as if we were casual friends because you can't figure out how to escape the calumny that is being heaped on your head paints you in the end not only to be lacking in guts, but also to be not a very nice person. At least you're not the person I thought you were. My fantasy man? I am not interested in rekindling my acquaintance with the person with whom I used to have heated, senseless debates over tea on the verandah.

*Instead of saying to me, "Me, I'm between a rock and a hard place here, what do you think I should do, what do you think would be the best solution here for the **both** of us?" you have apparently accepted the common herd's mantra of "Off with her head!" You seem to be allowing them to paint a portrait of me as the pursuer, the destroyer of a happy home when it was Mrs. that drew me into the web in the first place to relieve her own discomfort, and you later provided the silken threads of care and concern by which, in my utter desperation and despair I became more and more ensnared. You've been through this drama at least twice before in your life. Did you simply retreat with your hands in the air in surrender each time? It would appear that you are ready to do so again.*

If I hadn't been so strong and self sufficient and fiercely independent and all alone on my own for so many years (27 since my divorce), if I hadn't clenched my teeth and bore my isolation and utter loneliness for so long, if I wasn't so hopelessly ill now, then maybe I wouldn't have been drawn in as deeply and completely as I have been. "And if wishes were horses then beggars would ride."

Boy, oh boy. The woman that wrote that is righteously pissed! And a real head case to boot.

So this is how I started day one of "Nearing Completion," I-Ching Hexagram #64.

The situation is incomplete, but the chaos of the past is slowly giving way to order, and the goal is in sight. Nevertheless, you are still treading on thin ice. The way ahead is unobstructed, the goal is clear, but a cautious and careful attitude is still essential, lest you slip and fall.

— ©2014 Divination Foundation

*I*t now strikes me that I am really running out of food here having recently had to forestall the moneylenders on my house with a bucket-load of cash. As of today, I've lost 8lbs. over the last week or so. Almost 65 lbs. since the beginning of my illness a year ago. I'm fast approaching the magic number I had been maintaining in the years after college and just before I got pregnant with my daughter 36 years ago. Not sure if the current weight loss is due to further developments with my illness or simply to not eating enough. I still have a half box of crackers, white flour, a very little rice and some 5-minute oatmeal left as staples. No vegetables, but one grapefruit which I think at this point would burn a hole in my empty stomach. I do have a small tin of tuna (the thought of which makes me want to gag at the moment) and some canned salmon, the only light at the end of the hunger tunnel. On second thought, I could whip up a veritable feast. Still, not really very encouraging.

I'm having difficulty today with my food and my daily regimen of pills wanting to stay down once I swallow. Everything seems to start coming back up and gets stuck mid-way in my esophagus. (Something to tell my primary care physician or a gastroenterologist if I ever make it out of here to see one.) We'll see how desperate I get. The thing is, I have no money, no cash left for the next four days (really, can you believe it?), just the equivalent of 80 cents U.S. Mr. insisted, among other things, that I should never worry about food, ever. He'd take care of me. Just let him know what I needed. Go ahead, stretch myself financially if it comes to that. Keep pouring money that I arguably don't have into the house. He would keep me from falling. I can just hear the self-righteous Puritan-Work-Ethic types heaping blame upon me for the predicament I'm in. Throwing those first, second and third stones. I accept the blame. But I also know that there are others who would be willing to cut me a little slack, give me an emotional break. Those are the voices that I need in my head right now in order to keep going. Not the others.

Oh, wait! I just found some feta cheese for the crackers on hand. A tasty repast fit for a queen indeed. There is hope! Moments later the two crackers are starting to come back up. "And Still I Rise."

Amazing. When I first awoke this morning, I was actually beginning to experience some sense of relief at being free from the dependency on Mr. Real hunger could put an end to my resolve. Maybe I'm hallucinating. The nuclear option is still on the table.

A Final Recounting of the Major Interactions that Have Occurred between Mrs. and Me

*S*ince Mrs. seems to be telling her friends, at least according to Mr. —though I can't always trust his ability to recount details with bulletproof accuracy—that I am the *femme fatale* who has lured her loving husband astray, I feel the need for one last full and final summary of the sequence of major events chronicling our time together here on the estate. I somehow always feel the need to go back in time and match what actually transpired with what people think transpired on a fairly regular basis. Reality vs. fantasy. Get a real grip on how we got from there to here. Cause and effect. Who said what to whom and when. I want to own my own responsibility for my lot in life in general and my current situation at the moment in particular. Of course, we could all have made different choices at each juncture in our lives along the way. How easy to think so in the current moment, perhaps how much more difficult to have been able to do so at the time.

- When I first arrived at My Happy Retreat, Mrs. welcomed me with open arms and issued an open invitation to tea any day, everyday. No need to call. Just show up around 4:30 or 5 pm.

- She came to my apartment smiling and cupped my face in her hands, embraced me warmly and told me how happy she was to have me here. I marveled. It seemed as if we would be best friends for life. She continued to drop by from time to time seemingly glad for the female company in an environment overwhelmingly dominated by men.[1]

- She shared with me her fears about aging. "There is nothing worse than growing old," she said on more than one occasion. I repeated my mother's words, "Consider the alternative." But in retrospect that response must have seemed so horribly flip to someone for whom growing old was indeed the worst thing that could happen. "Do you want to know what hell on earth really is?" she said. "Growing old."

- She talked about not wanting to wear sleeveless blouses because of her slightly sagging underarms.

- She told not only me but the maid and Mr. as well that if she ever started to lose her mind to Alzheimer's or any form of dementia that she wanted to be put out of her misery. (People who suffer from clinical depression have a greater risk of going that route.) She didn't want to live if she weren't in full command of her faculties.

- I came to tea. Sometimes I called to let her know I was coming over, sometimes she called me to tell me to come. I was aware of not wanting to wear out my welcome, but she continued to call and invite me when I didn't show up for a few days.

- After I got my own car, from time to time I asked if she wanted a ride to the grocery store in town since she had offered the same to me when I was without one. For the most part, before I was able to rescue my car from the customs officials on the wharf, I had depended upon a limo service to take me because I did not want to be dependent or take advantage of her graciousness. I needed a driver several cuts above the average taxi man in case my life-long bouts with anxiety should cause me problems on my various treks around the island.

- Mrs. is a die-hard shopper, a shopaholic, I am not. I absolutely loathe shopping. (I've mentioned this before I think. It seems to me to be important information for the reader to know.) When I drove the two of us into Tourist Town, I would end up waiting in the car for her while she finished. I took something to read. Eventually, she said that she felt guilty making me wait and eventually ended up declining my invitations for a ride.

- Sometimes Mrs. and I had time alone to have a friendly chat on the verandah of the Great House, two women sharing the personal details of their lives, before Mr. arrived for tea. She began to tell me more about her life with him. I think she felt comfortable because he and I would have knock down drag out arguments on the topic of the day—whatever it was—politics, philosophy, you name it we were at odds about it. I became a kindred spirit, someone with whom she could share the adversarial aspects of her life with Mr. We became friends.

- I learned that he could be unbearably judgmental and demanding and capable of launching a verbal tirade at a moment's notice. She told me that once, when she hadn't finished cleaning a spot on the verandah and he chanced upon the as yet unfinished task, he berated her mercilessly and demanded, over and over again, why she hadn't finished the job in its entirety, why she had allowed herself to be distracted mid-stream from completing the job. Why? Why? Why? I subsequently came to experience that relentless pounding myself. Bizarre. Definitely a psychological quirk.

- She told me that years before in London, she had opened a personal bank account in which she made small deposits from her paycheck on a routine basis. On one occasion, when there was a financial shortfall in the household one month, she proudly told him that she would be able to help out by making a withdrawal from her savings. But he went ballistic. She was stunned. She cried. He was relentless in his attack on her for hiding something that important from him, by keeping vital information to herself. This obviously reeked of control issues on his part. But in the end, it made her fearful and ever more secretive to the extent that she now had secret bank accounts in multiple locations here in Tourist Town and a neighboring town as well. She even had her own credit cards about which he had no knowledge when I first arrived on the scene.

- She became furtive in her trips to the various bank locations where her different stashes were hidden. I learned about them during the period of time when we would make trips to the grocery store or my bank together. I was urged to maintain the secrecy because of the trauma that had ensued years before in London and how his all-out verbal and emotional assault had hurt her, shook her to the core. She thought she had done something wonderful, a welcome surprise. She had never meant to hide something vital, something crucial from him. The experience was a powerful lesson in how to be and how not to be around him. She learned to be secretive and to keep certain information from him. She made it clear that this event had a powerful effect on the rest of her life and how she dealt with him. Pernicious.

- She reminded me not just once, or twice, but on several occasions that Mr. was a "girly man." The first time she said it, I had to ask her to repeat the phrase because I had never heard it used to describe a man in terms other than what I thought truly did not apply to him. She explained it referred to a man who liked women. In other words he enjoyed the company of women as friends.

- She also told me on more than one occasion that knowing he was a "girly man," she had told him that he could have women as friends but that he just couldn't sleep with them, and she referenced two women whom I knew as examples. She said that her friends had told her when she and he first started dating to beware the fact that he was a girly man, but she assured them she could deal with it by giving him some latitude.

- On numerous occasions during our tea time debates, I stood up for her opinions when he would put them down. I asked her to voice her thoughts when he talked over her attempts to pronounce her ideas about a given topic. I became her ally over the months and years and she clearly saw me as such and was appreciative. I was her friend.

- At one point she shared with me the fact that she hadn't been away on holiday off the island for a couple of years and that she longed to visit her children and their families abroad. She particularly enjoyed London with its endless shopping opportunities and theatres, and she could easily live there for the rest of her life.

- She complained to me about his demanding to have lunch ready at a certain time and then not showing up until later because he was out and about on the property. She also complained about his sometimes coming in for a meal earlier than expected and flouncing out when he discovered the meal wasn't ready yet. What she was describing to me was a woman on tenterhooks, never quite able to please the man in charge.

- She complained that he didn't compliment her on her cooking but when he was unimpressed by or disappointed in a particular meal he would let her know, and she felt that her efforts at trying to be creative or innovative or nurturing were unappreciated and, indeed, of little to no value in his eyes.

- She told me that he never gave her signs of affection—such as a passing touch on the arm—or addressed her with terms of endearment. Indeed, she told me one of his sister's told her words to the effect that "Oh yes, he may not show it, but he really appreciates all that you do for him." She seemed grateful for that acknowledgement from someone in his family. On a much later occasion he himself remarked to me that that was indeed the case, and I understood him to mean that his recounting of the circumstances of their unplanned, "necessity" marriage was the reason behind what amounted to his lack of romantic enthusiasm or tender feelings towards her. He was not in love with her, had never been in love with her. Theirs was a marriage borne of social necessity not one borne of love, and while there was commitment and loyalty to the marriage on his part—he would never leave her high and dry—the piece of paper that signified their union in the eyes of society and the law could never dictate the true feelings of his heart.

- She told me that his mother never liked her and had accused her of "all sorts of things." It wasn't until near the end of the mother's life when she became more and more reliant on the assistance of others to get through the day, that she finally relented and had to accept the necessary ministrations of Mrs.

- She indicated to me that she longed for a break from having to fix the major mid-day meal everyday for Mr. at a certain time. That she longed for the opportunity not to get dressed until the middle of the day if she so desired or have cheese and crackers for a meal rather than having to prepare a full menu. I took that to mean that if the opportunity for a break from those duties and his demands associated with it arose, she would not only be grateful but would relish the opportunity to be her own person in her own home for an extended period of time.

- She told me that she hated the fact that the workers on the farm could come up to the kitchen door or front door or front verandah at will or that somebody could just walk or drive into the front yard up to her very doorstep. After 20 years in residence, she was just now speaking up about not having enough privacy. It took three years from the time that conversation took place for the doors to the Great House and the gate to the front yard to be closed and the workers instructed to come only to the kitchen door.

- She told me that Mr. was completely in charge of the remodeling of the house and that when she had requested window seats in the living room and master bedroom, he refused because he thought them a waste of space. He called the shots. She told me that he chastised any efforts that she made in the garden. She made it clear in every communication that Mr. was in control of everything having to do with My Happy Retreat and she had little or no say. I thought it patently unfair, unnatural, not right. The house was the woman's domain. As her friend, as a woman, I felt her anguish, I felt her unease. I understood that the events and feelings that she was describing, among others, were behind the reason that she later seemed to completely withdraw into the confines of the house, upstairs sifting through stored clothing from decades past. When both Mr. and Mrs. independently told me about the pathological control that her mother had exercised over her while growing up, it seemed to be all part of a lifetime pattern of being the submissive to the dominants in her primary relationships. I felt sad for her and empathized with her suffering.

- When Mrs. chose to no longer accompany me or even Mr. and me on my few business related trips into Capital City, I assumed that she was simply enjoying the respite that being away from the demands of Mr. were being afforded to her. I envisioned her relaxing, not dressing until the afternoon, eating crackers and cheese (that favorite of the woman on her own!) when and where she felt like it. And I truly believed then that was indeed the case. But maybe not so much now? Maybe it was during one of those times when his absence gave her the opportunity to explore her possibilities for being, that she began retreating into a world of fantasy and fear preparing to remake herself into some new image of who she used to be, of what she thought she should be, of what she and Mr. would soon be together once the property was sold and they could leave their happy retreat.

Months later she would eventually begin a compulsive regimen of diet and exercise that she thought would bring about a renaissance in her appeal to him and in their relationship. Meanwhile, oblivious to her growing fears related to aging, to not enjoying the same level of camaraderie with her husband as I did, to thinking that a slimmer body, a more appealing outfit would render her more desirable, Mr. and I became more adventurous in the quality and visibility of the establishments where we chose to have lunch, and I took pleasure in the opportunity to wear my own lovely clothes. Mr. and I were noticed. We were a stunning couple. A few months before all of the drama occurred, when we were dining at a Who's Who of luncheon establishments, she called to remind him of her existence in the world. We had been seen. Phone calls had been made. A relay of calls from one end of the island to the other. I should have known better to try to stand out, but I was heady, deliriously intoxicated by a sense of belonging at long last. For a brief few months, I was no longer alone, isolated, cast adrift as I am once again now. I was his Woman. Post-feminist style.

• I first began to see for myself that things changed between Mrs. and me when she came back from her first trip to the U.K. to visit her son 3 ½ years after I arrived at My Happy Retreat. Instead of the front and kitchen doors that faced my apartment being open all day long they were now closed. I was shut out. A barricade erected to my presence. This was months before the crisis in my illness and Mr.'s intervention in my life. Instead of there being a perpetual open door policy for tea and conversation, I maybe went to the Great House 3 or 4 times for that whole year. On the few occasions when I called about coming over, I was mostly told that that day wouldn't be convenient. He was out in the field and she wasn't sure when he would be back. I told her that she and I alone could chat and have tea but it didn't seem to work out. I had no idea why. I was being totally cut off from the companionship of the only other female on the property, from the person whom I had come to see as my friend and the person whose cause I had come to champion.

After the relationship with Mr. grew into something more several months after I had come back from the hospital in Miami, I remarked to Mr. that for the almost the whole year I had not been invited for tea. He seemed surprised, but I hardly believed that he really could be because the change was in such stark contrast to what had gone on before. There had been a demonstrable difference in her attitude towards me after she had come back from England in the early spring. I didn't know why. I still don't know what caused it. I speculate that perhaps she had gotten tired of the tension generated by the debates over politics, etc. and just wanted to keep herself to herself.

- The closed door policy and the renunciation of what had been the tea time tradition continued over the ensuing months. And now she tells me that right after she had come back to visit her son in Leeds for the second time, she could see that my attitude towards HER had changed? She had returned the evening before I left to go to the hospital in Miami. I was dying, unable to breathe due to congestive heart failure. But she has told Mr. that she thinks on the morning of my departure I wasn't attentive or excited enough on seeing her for the first time in about two months of being away in England with a broken arm! I was dying, literally gasping for each breath, struggling to stay alive and yet I wasn't sufficiently excited about seeing her again! Could she possibly really have said something as insanely self-centered as that?!! That's his account of her characterization of the event.

- She has also explained to me that she continues to feel justified in having barred me from having access to the doctor who performed the routine medical procedure on Mr. on the scheduled day even though Mr. had specifically asked me to be present to talk to him. I asked, "Even if it potentially put Mr.'s life in danger because I wasn't able to remind the doctor about an important issue of concern regarding the use of a sedative?" "Yes" was her answer. "Because I'm his wife and that's my job."

I continue to remain the intruder, the interloper, the aggressor into her wifely domain. If there was any information to have been conveyed, she should have been the one to convey it! But when I'm the one with specific background knowledge, how do I have that conversation third hand? I was the one who had made all of the arrangements! I was the one who had been having an on-going dialogue with the doctor the nature of which she could never have been capable of initiating or sustaining. She had been confined to the second floor of the house, too busy trying to transform both herself and her wardrobe, involved in who knows what aspect of her personal ministrations to see to her husband's medical needs.

There is still at least one medical procedure that he desperately needs to have performed. That's what a wife is supposed to see to for her husband. Make sure the important stuff is taken care of. Men of a certain age sometimes do not to attend to these things themselves (a sexist, ageist stereotype I know). But she's been too busy with her alterations. Or maybe it's her crosswords. Or maybe it's the housework or mudpacks. But his vision will eventually be impaired if somebody doesn't act. But it clearly won't be me. Who is it that said, "Walk softly and carry a big stick?" My footfalls were too heavy and my magic wand too small. I must no longer be concerned about his general welfare. Constantly on my mind is the question of who I can find to be concerned about mine.

• She told me the other day that she thinks that I deliberately set out to embarrass her at the math and science community-building event organized by Mr. and myself. Astounding! Especially when I thought that both her refusal to participate and her refusal to sit apart from the main activity was clearly an act of passive aggression on her part. (And if one of the participants indeed approached her and said, "Why aren't you sitting with the rest of the group?" isn't it because she chose to place herself conspicuously in full view of the comings and goings yet slightly apart from everyone else prompting such an inquiry of polite concern?) She has clearly been experiencing some degree of paranoia and is filtering her interpretation of life's events solely in terms of how they play into her illusions about reality with no concern for the actual role that others are playing in helping to shape it. But surely such a self-centered perception can be clearly attributed to an upbringing in which Mrs. was the sole focus of her mother's total exercise of authority and control over her daughter's life?

In the last years of her life, it would seem that Mrs. is apparently reliving her childhood as a helpless prisoner in a world where she was the *ens causa sui*, her mother's *raison d'etre*. It was all about her yet it wasn't about her at all. It was really about the Grand Puppet Mistress, at once both visible and invisible, behind the curtain yet there in plain sight, manipulating both puppet and audience, pulling the strings while the puppet, brightly clad, dances and sings and entertains the audience with refreshments to be served before, during and after the performance.

Something for everyone! A comedy tonight!

And, indeed, is that not how she has lived her entire life, making sure that it has always been all about her whenever possible? Whether on the stage or in her personal life? In the way she dresses, in the way she flutters around her guests, in the way she caters to and tolerates Mr.'s more egregious displays of berating and belittling? The former brings her applause from one and all. The latter ensures her enshrinement as the long-suffering, dedicated wife. Look at what she has put up with for all of these years! And on top of the infidelities! It serves to cement her place in the Martyr-to-the-Cause Hall of Fame.

And that stance has served her well because now her friends rally around her, indeed as they should, but fail to see her depression, fail to see her role in scripting the drama of her making now unfolding. And Mr. retreats into the submissive posture of the canine with his four legs in the air in the presence of authority, ready to obey commands.

TONI M. FORSYTH

She seems to me to be the *petit* narcissist who sees reflected in every surface dull or shiny an image of herself. If the reflection is one with which she is not pleased, then it must be erased. Maybe that's what really happened to our friendship. I had been reflecting back an image of her as someone who had been incapable of standing up for herself, a victim. My whole life, lived by myself, in support of myself, standing up against a perceived injustice and for the rights of others when and where I could was in such contrast to how she had chosen to live her life that she came to realize that Mr., despite the often debilitating knock-down-drag-out debates in which we had engaged, actually admired who I was. She told me once that she knew he really liked me.

Liked how? I know not how,
As if...

More than a year ago Mrs. retreated into the confines of her house for months on end only to re-emerge in the role that I recently described to Mr. as that of a sword-wielding harridan seeing in me the enemy intent on disrupting her world when in fact I thought I had fallen into synchrony with the world she had constructed. But she has now defined a new role for herself and Mr. apparently can do nothing else but fall in line with it. How odd that these two are now scripting a decidedly different final act to be played out before they go gently into that good night. All I can do is retreat from the fray. I don't think I'll be able to stick around long enough to watch it play itself out.

(From the Notes of Dr. Peterson)

From all accounts, these journal entries represent an accurate account of events as they transpired involving the principal residents of the Paradise Island plantation known as My Happy Retreat. The details have been independently corroborated. The commentary and analysis of those events enhance our under-standing of the journal entries penned by "Me."

August 25th

*M*r. phoned to tell me that he had called my cousin at the other end of the island out of concern for me. I responded with anger telling him he had no right to do so. I reiterated that I had no relatives and no friends who had any substantive concern for or any material involvement in my life. He knew from our conversation the night before that I was beyond upset with the "Can't we just be friends?" request he had proffered in response to the chaos swirling about since Mrs. told her friends about her blood pressure and now possible heart problems caused by the direct threat to her marriage that I posed and the tense stand-off that had developed at My Happy Retreat because of the relationship that had developed between Mr. and myself. I was the Enemy, the Other Woman: Every married woman's worst nightmare.

It didn't matter that her daily routines, her anticipated life in the U.K., the quality and frequency of her interactions with Mr. would not change in any material way (he was actually being nicer to her) by the continuing "presence" of me in their lives. The illusion of their marriage would not change. It was the "reality" of me and what I represent that is causing her to panic. I need to wrap my head around that. It means that illusion is as important as reality. It means that real world consequences can be the same for both. It means that Plato's realm of Ideas can deliver up the same number of dead bodies as Aristotle's quantifiable tangibles. The pen and the sword can kill with equal precision. Real happiness is not in the cards: only life and death.

He wanted to know if there was anything that he could do, anything he could say, anybody he could call to intervene on my behalf in a palliative capacity because I told him I was prepared to end my life when I felt the time was right. I was not well and not getting any better. The fantasy of my having so much to live for was his not mine. Yes, I had a lot to offer. But no, I was determined to regain control of my personal life by cutting him loose, and as my symptoms multiplied, I wasn't about to pledge any part of it again to the indignities of a prolonged illness spent in isolation from him much less fall prey to the whims and caprices of other people's insanities or personal agendas.

From: *Me*
To: *Mr.*
Sent: *Friday, August 25th, 12:36 PM*
Subject: *What You Can Do*

1) You can get your wife to go back and retract what she has said and stop telling people that I am trying to take you away from her. She never had you, not really. She had already established herself beginning in the spring of last year as a) wanting to be shut away in the house mending clothes or doing housework or cooking or doing crosswords or watching television or reading novels; and b) preferring the life she led in the U.K., especially London. In the past she had no problem being away from you and the plantation for months on end. My existence did not threaten anything that she had not already posed for herself. It only made tangible that which was already visible to any who cared enough to look.

2) Get a grip on your life and be able to articulate what it is you really want out of what time you've got left on this earth because at one point it sounded as if you really wanted to take charge of where you were headed. The reality being played out here is that you are allowing yourself to be led around by the nose not only by Mrs. but by Friend Gerald and company. How can you let these lesser lights dictate to you?!! The Mr. that I am now seeing is not the one with whom I became friends, who was strong and masterful, and with whom I became enamored. But perhaps it is just now that I am seeing the real you, the one who is comfortable with only half a glass, the one that I couldn't see before because of my rose colored glasses.

*3) Please tell me who are you really, what do you want out of the rest of your life and are you willing to take back control and realize the possibilities yet to come? And that doesn't mean flushing Mrs. down the toilet either. It never was about that, but it sounds to me as if you may be so busy wallowing in guilt or a mistaken concern for the self-righteous opinion of others (Gerald comes to mind)—or something—that you aren't really trying to **make yourself heard** and get the message across to her as well as to everyone else because hers is the convoluted lens through which all communications are now being funneled—that you are more than you currently are. She is clearly indulging her own fantasy fueled by a sense of victimhood, but you are the only one who is around who could try to bring her and eventually everyone else who has bought in to the illusion and stuck his or her finger into the toxic pie she has concocted back to some semblance of reality. Do you want to define yourself as the person locked up inside that big house on Sugar Loaf Hill or the person wandering around the old haunts of London trying to find something meaningful, anything at all to even temporarily engage his mind?*

(What do you have to feel guilty about anyway? She's the one that manipulated you into a loveless marriage by deliberately getting pregnant 2 months before you were set to leave for university in the U.K. Did you murder someone in Zimbabwe and Mrs. knows where the body is buried and the gun is stashed?)

Maybe you have become transfixed in a quagmire of accumulated guilt about which I can only guess. I really have no clue. If you are, it is possible to get out. I cannot seriously believe that you are willing to let yourself be held hostage to these people—your Circle of Frendz—and Mrs. Anybody else who is even vaguely aware of what's going on in our lives is just being dragged along for the ride, couldn't care less and would rather be just about anywhere else on God's green earth than in the middle of this grand drama, this dance for two (or three) that she has choreographed. But this is where I may be seriously deluded. I would love a definitive answer. Or perhaps you have already given me your final word and I am willfully engaging in one last desperate attempt to indulge my own fantasy of "Say it ain't so, Joe! Say it ain't so!"

But above all else, first and foremost, tell me who you really are. Or even who you really want to be while you still have the time to be that person. Who are you? What do you want out of life?

TONI M. FORSYTH

Have I bashed her enough? I guess so. Have I made my point? More than sufficiently. Have I been wallowing unbecomingly in my own *mishegas?* You betcha! Has my analysis of cause and effect been plausible? No question. Have I vindicated myself? Time to move on.

We talked on the phone last night at length—me from my bed in my apartment, he parked at my house enjoying the solitude of the stunning view and the cool night air. He says I know who he is, he hasn't changed. He's still the same person. I say he has changed. The person I thought I knew was dynamic and take-charge, could use his famous management skills and rational brain to get things back on track. He wasn't like the dog that rolls over on its back with his four legs in the air when the dominant male walks past his kennel. I say it's the difference between the crucifix in the Catholic church that leaves the Christ figure hanging on the cross memorializing suffering and sacrifice and martyrdom and pain, and the crucifix in the Protestant church where the Christ figure has been removed denoting ascendancy over pain and suffering and death. "He is risen!"

August 26th:
(Draft of E-mail Not Sent to Mr.)

From: Me
To: Mr.
Sent: Not
Subject: Emergency Room?

You've always demanded to know the truth. Here it is:

1. *The result of my calling my primary care doctor, your cousin's daughter, in order to make an appointment to find out what to do about my shortness of breath was an unbelievably cruel, sarcastic and tragically caustic response on her part for me to "go suck lime, garlic and onions" ostensibly to treat what is ailing me. That is not just unkind but speaks to a lack of personal integrity on the part of a physician, a lack of empathy in relation to another human being and a kind of pathology of the spirit. But I remember that she grew up in a household where the mother beat her developmentally disabled brother for not doing well enough in school. Hers is a learned sickness of the heart and of the soul.*

2. *The result of your unsolicited call to my cousin on the other end of the island merely served to confirm for you (because I already knew) that I have no relatives who are concerned about what happens to me. I simply ended up reverberating from the brute force and unnerving sound of yet another nail being pounded into my coffin.*

3. *The result of whatever is going wrong with my body is that I have been telling you daily that I am constantly having difficulty with a) finding food palatable; b) the contents of my stomach wanting to come back up; c) feeling like there's a furnace heating up inside of me; d) periodically experiencing episodes where my skin feels cold and clammy; e) sweat*

TONI M. FORSYTH

pouring down from the top of my head; and f) not feeling well enough to stay out of bed for more than a few minutes at a time. All of this in spite of Dr. Local who thinks what I really need is to see a hairdresser and go pamper myself. That's sexism as plain as day and it comes at the expense of my life. Why haven't you taken the initiative to recommend that we go to the University Hospital. Oh, I forgot. You've been required to put the kibosh on any display of concern for my well-being.

4. *The result of my current state of health is that I do believe that I may, in fact, be dying. Slowly. Bit by bit. That is what my body is telling me. When I wrote to my cardiologist, he saw fit to begin his inquires by requesting I take a newly developed blood test to determine whether or not I was in the throes once again of congestive heart failure.*

5. *The result of my conveying this information to you is that not once have you expressed concern regarding this growing body of symptoms or seen fit to suggest taking me to another doctor or the University ER to find out what's wrong, because something is obviously very seriously wrong with me that needs immediate attention.*

I have been mistaking you for who I thought you were. Yesterday you helped me to clarify who you really are now. Fantasy versus reality. This is why I cannot have you around me. I cannot be distracted by the fantasy of what you once were (or maybe what I once thought you were in the process of becoming). At this point you have become irrelevant, unnecessary, perhaps an actual detriment to my well being because I've been waiting around for you to take some control of my downwardly spiraling health situation instead of stepping forward to take action on my own although there's not really much I can personally do at this point.

I keep telling you the house is not my life and is of no interest to me any more. It is a monstrous distraction. You keep saying that you know me but how could you when you're not hearing what I'm telling you? You obviously don't know me, not really. You are no longer who you previously were in my life and trying to interact with a fantasy does me more harm than good. The fantasy keeps me hanging on longer than I should. I must take back control of my life in the only way that I now can.

I have 68 pills. Will I be able to keep them all down?

I dared not send this as originally written. His response the next day to a highly truncated version of this document? "I am who I have always been."

Obviously I could not send this e-mail. Talk about wallowing in self-pity! Talk about emotional blackmail and sending him off to call for the nearest padded wagon! No, no, no. This won't do at all.

Funny thing though. When I started composing this message the impulse in me to follow through with the pills seemed totally appropriate and justifiable. The urge still comes in the middle of the night even days later. Was it the act of writing in and of itself that changed my perspective on mailing the letter or doing the deed? or did simply time-on-task dull the impulse? Before I started writing, I was actually gripping the pill bottle quite firmly in my hand and thinking about Robin Williams and what he must have been thinking when he put the belt around his neck. Why choose such a prolonged and frightening and painful death? But then again, as I mentioned earlier, his whole *shtick* was about thrashing and flailing about. Mine has been about keeping still until the discomfort subsides in the hopes that I won't throw up and make a mess. I'm all about containment.

What do I do next?

Who exactly is running off the rails here at My Happy Retreat? Easy answer. The two women. Geriatric depression, anxiety, panic, etc. The over 65 set, senior citizens, in the past simply didn't talk about what they were going through or enough people didn't listen or didn't care or both. Now that the doctors and researchers themselves are geriatric cases, lo and behold an important new field of study has arisen where

Do not go gentle into that good night...
Rage, rage against the dying of the light.

has become the mantra of the day. The changes that come with old age speak to the loss of independence and ever-increasing dependence on others to do, eventually, the most basic of human tasks. It's the loss of the person we defined ourselves as being. Even the mirror tells us we're not the same person. And the person that we are at any given moment is sometimes changing with frightening speed.

It starts with someone having to balance the checkbook for you, then physically write out the checks, and eventually spoon feed the food that was bought from the proceeds of those checks into the mouths of those who can no longer hold a fork, much less add up numbers or write with a pen. And that's if we live long enough to get to that stage. My mother, who lived to be 102, believed up until the day she died of what? old age?—no specific ailment—that she didn't need anyone to take care of her, that she just needed a little assistance, just a helping hand getting in and out of bed and into her motorized wheelchair which she could have really manage all on her own given enough time to do so. And she probably could have up until the night that she drifted off to sleep and didn't wake up. But my mother was an extraordinary human being. She was who she always was up until the very end.

I wanted to take charge of the last third of my life. Instead I have become so mired in circumstances that at this point are so far beyond my immediate control that I have cut that third by at least two thirds if not much more. My happy retreat into retirement—envisioned complete with selfless service to the local community in which I live as my parting gift to the world—has become my unhappy nightmare mired in debt and major illness threatening to lock me down for good. All the things that seemed so right at first, so promising to begin with have ended up on the scrap heap of good intentions gone bad.

I watched an Amy Winehouse video a couple of days ago taped during a live performance, and at the end she grinned happily at the audience and said in her wonderful accent, "We're still alive! Still alive! Still standin'!"

https://www.youtube.com/watch?v=362JArvhAqg&list =PLHDbggXt_6xvN863-kUGPUNRMf7jDOGYQ&index=29

We all know how that turned out. But then again, her circumstances are so completely different from mine I guess it's not worth even a fleeting comparison.

September 1st:
Consorting with the Enemy

He called me last night while he was out jogging/walking. It's the only time he's not in danger of her listening in. I asked him if he wanted me to step outside, to join him for a moment at the end. He said no, that he was afraid. My God! He was afraid of her. So it's come to this.

He was in need of consoling, of connection. He had spent almost the whole day running a seemingly endless series of errands with her—errands she, of course, could have run on her own, but now she wants him by her side so that everyone knows that she's the wife. He is obliging her.

He was sad about the death of a nephew last week who had been in a nursing home, almost completely paralyzed by a stroke for almost two years. He started reminiscing about another relative about whom he had "forgotten." I didn't have the faintest idea what he was going on and on about. I was being dumped *in media res* into ancient family history. He said something about my being able to understand why I was the one he wanted to call and talk to about all of the feelings he was experiencing. I said yes, that I understood why. I began to get the warm fuzzies and felt sympathetic, empathetic. It turns out he has yet another nephew, the out-of-wedlock son of a relative from another unsanctioned liaison. The guy is living in Australia and wanted to be remembered during the funeral services as part of the family. Mr. also started talking some nonsense about the need for me to "hold my head high." I told him I didn't know what he was talking about. He started rambling on mentioning the so-called Circle of Frendz who were bad-mouthing me: most likely Bernie and Pepper. I told him that I despised those people and that they meant nothing to me, so it had never even crossed my mind that I had anything to be concerned about or any reason to hold my head in a position other than where it had always been.

His rambling bothered me. He told me that he would be getting the name of a taxi driver from Bernie who could drive me into the city for not much money. I told him I didn't want the name of a taxi driver especially from a sworn enemy because I already had a driver that I'd had for years who I trusted to be able to look after me if I became ill. Concerned about his state of mind, I asked if we could have a bit of time the following day to chat before he went off to the States for five days to attend his nephew's funeral. He said yes.

September 2nd:
"Comfort Woman"

*H*e called this morning wanting to give me the name of the taxi driver and a psychotherapist (disturbed individual that I am) that Bernie had recommended. I was furious. I reminded him that I had told him the night before that I didn't want the name of a taxi driver and that I didn't want the name of a therapist either. He kept insisting. I told him no and hung up. I called him back almost immediately and told him that I was really upset that he would try to insist on giving me that information. He kept at it over and over again. He gets into these mind loops sometimes—an interesting brain processing quirk. I could be charitable and say that he actually thought he was trying to help me, but I believe at least the proximate reason for the *quid pro quo* is that he was trying to assuage his guilt for using me as his "comfort woman." Because that's what I was last night. But I won't be that again.

He knows how to connect with and run to me whenever he's in need of an emotional boost, but he can't figure out how to maintain a connection that fits in with my needs. He has a mind that is pragmatic, goal oriented and seeks to find solutions to immediate problems. But that is not the kind of mind that necessarily serves a romantic partner in good stead during times of great emotional upheaval. He is oblivious to the fact that supplying the name of a body that can drive me into the city for a doctor's appointment is not what I need. Once again he has insulted me to the core and he hasn't a clue why. If I get the chance, and if I am so motivated, I will try to explain it to him.

TONI M. FORSYTH

Mr., in the company of Mrs., now consorts with my enemies, dines at the table of my enemies and in so doing gives aid and comfort to my enemies. He is literally sleeping with my enemy—the woman who has identified me as her enemy in order to find a scapegoat for her own deteriorating identity.

"A Moral Universe:" An Essay by The Author

I believe that we live in a moral universe, and that somewhere down the line we will be asked to account for our actions. And when that time comes, we will be held to account for our transgressions in one way or another. I believe that our greatest fears begin to be realized in the moment when we become aware that the willful harm (malignant harm) we have caused our fellow man has been noted. For example, if a person is in fear of not having friends, and she betrays the trust of a particular friend in order to ingratiate herself with another (or other) friends in order to curry favour—believing the gossip that she spreads will elevate her status in the eyes of others—then she will ultimately be known to both friend and foe alike as an untrustworthy person. In the end, she will be shunned by all for her true nature will have been exposed for everyone to see.

Another example of how one's greatest fears may come to fruition as a consequence of accountability within the universe arises when someone draws another person into a triangle of manipulation for selfish ends. A case in point is when a wife (Mrs.?) discloses information about problems that exist within her marriage to a friend (Me?) which highlights the fact that the wife is living in a situation where she is decidedly subservient to her husband (Mr.?). The unwitting friend eventually becomes the third party witness to the ongoing domestic drama which routinely unfolds before her and experiences herself as being placed in the position of having to stand up for the wife in the face of any domineering or oppressive behaviour on the part of the husband to which she is privy. The friend is destined for

TONI M. FORSYTH

a double whammy because in many such cases both husband and wife eventually turn on the friend, each for their own not-always-so-obvious reasons. It is at that point that all three become aware that a distinct harm, a willful harm, a malignant harm has occurred.

Who then is to be held to account for the initiating behaviour in a situation such as this? The wife for ostensibly making a not-so-silent plea for help in a long-standing difficult situation? The husband for being insensitive to his wife's sensibilities? The friend for interfering while thinking she is being supportive?

In this instance I believe the greatest degree of accountability lies with the wife who subsequently castigates, marginalizes and finally denigrates her friend for having interfered in the dynamics of the intimate relationship between husband and wife. The wife gets to enjoy the fruits of a now more sensitized husband and the husband gets the benefit of a more appreciative wife. The friend is left having been manipulated into playing the role of the instigator rather than the liberator.

Clearly the wife acted neither honestly nor forthrightly in the circumstances. Her friend was set up from the beginning to take the fall. Because the wife chose not to act honestly and directly on her own behalf, she could never be blamed by the husband for challenging his authority. Add to this the fact that the wife actively encouraged a genuinely close relationship between the husband and the friend by having them spend hours and hours of time alone together thereby supposedly giving the wife a break from her household duties and some time to herself, and one can see a stage set by a director choreographing the movements, pulling the strings and yanking the chains of the lives of the people she sought to control for her own totally self serving ends.

What nightmare scenario might the universe serve up that would allow the wife to be held accountable for her actions? An older woman's innate fear of growing old, of losing her looks, of losing her husband and ending up alone? A recognized fear of one day losing her mental faculties so that she could no longer stealthily manipulate the people in her life in order to maintain some form of control? These indeed might be the avenues that the universe spotlights in order to balance the forces that allow us all to exist in relation to one another, hopefully with some modicum of harmony and peace.

But what then of the husband and the friend? Are there no accounts to be held by either of them? Let's look at the motivation of each.

The friend became part of the triangle thinking that she might even be performing a good deed—a *mitzvah*. She spoke up in the face of oppression, belligerence and intolerance. Where she erred was in allowing herself to get carried off into a relationship with the husband that was not hers for the having no matter how prettily it was packaged or how nicely it was offered up on a silver platter for her consumption. A rookie mistake. A benign, but not a malignant error on her part. Not willful harm. As for the husband, he had been down this road before with other women who had been shepherded one way or another into his path by his wife who actually thought if she offered up an occasional sacrifice, he would be more appreciative and forgiving of her in the end. His error was more egregious because he knew, knowing her, and knowing himself, what the final outcome would be.

His fear now destined to be lived? Two-fold: 1) that his autonomous life would end. That from now on he would forever be monitored and shepherded from one mindless task to another, subjected to endless chatter at home, in the car, wherever—"a tale told by an idiot, signifying nothing"—otherwise the wife would threaten to kill herself in retaliation by willing herself to have a stroke, burst a blood vessel, blow an aneurysm; and 2) his dwindling resources would dissipate further because the good energy and good fortune that was generated by being in a mutually supportive relationship between equals, by doing good works, by caring about the welfare of others in addition to one's own had been cast to the four winds while pursuing an ultimately self-centered end and not keeping the well-being of another at the forefront of his thoughts.

God requires of us that we take the welfare of others into account. The husband was required to be his friend's keeper. Once again, like Camus' school teacher, he couldn't not choose to do so. He couldn't just let things

TONI M. FORSYTH

slide. One is required to choose. One is required to act. Inaction is action. No decision is a decision. In the end, he left his new friend as he found her—alone—but more alone than before and for that he will have to atone. So the good energy they previously generated when together will no longer be around to help him soar. It cannot be destroyed, but it will not manifest itself in the same way it once did. And that is a real loss.

And finally, the friend's fear that will be lived out? That she will end up once again alone because the path that leads one time and time again to intervene on behalf of others ultimately leads to unbearable isolation. Speaking up in the face of injustice is more often than not a solitary pursuit. There are few who would risk being able to bask in the glow of good fellowship and camaraderie because they chose not to stand up against those who would intimidate the more vulnerable among us. What was self-centered on her part was going the extra step, taking the leap into thinking that the wife wanted real relief, not just a temporary holiday. And what was not necessarily willful harm but assuredly self-centeredness and self-indulgence on her part, and that for which she must be held to some measure of accountability was believing that the role she had been scripted to perform in the little domestic drama would play itself out differently from times past. Because she had been warned in advance. She had previously been told the story. The principal characters were already cast in stone decades before she met up with them. The third *dramatis personae* may have changed costumes but the part she played from beginning to end remained the same. And for that, she would pay. More of the same.

Fix-Its

*M*y generation thinks we'll fix it all. Fix everything our parents screwed up. Everything they got wrong. Everything they couldn't see because they were too old, too out of it, too set in their ways, too blind to the ways of the world that was rapidly changing around them. We Boomer's won't age, we won't get sick, we won't die. And if we do start to age or get sick despite all of the cleverly designed exercise regimens and the cosmetic "lifestyle lifts" and the organic foods and the spiritual and sexual healing, we'll fix whatever's wrong. One of us, with all of his or her advanced degrees and spiritual enlightenment and self awareness will figure out the answer, find the cure, make things once again like they were. All we have to do is dream a dream for ourselves then go make it happen. That was the promise. That's what we believe. That's how we will continue to live our lives until the day we die. And that death will be far away in the distant future. We just have to make sure we have the magic elixir, the right organic compound and "Follow the directions as prescribed."

At the very least that is our ongoing fantasy. It may turn out to be the reality for some of us. But certainly not for all of us who are still around. Some of us will end up retreating one way or another (as have Mr. and Mrs. who actually don't qualify as Boomers), into the comfort (or profound discomfort) of the complex illusion become reality with which we have grown accustomed until something threatens it. And then whoever has the reins firmly in hand will give them a tug and make it so that things are once again pulled back toward some semblance of a center which, at all costs,

TONI M. FORSYTH

must hold. People buy into the program—whatever the program—at an early age and seem willing to hold on to it because it is familiar, and the familiar is almost always better, safer, certainly more secure than the unknown.

Both Mr. and Mrs. are willing to continue to co-exist at what I would have thought to be a profoundly unsatisfactory level. But they each, independently of each other, vowed to themselves that they were in it for the long haul no matter what. She could have been happy in London attending the theatre, doing her thing, endlessly shopping and enjoying the company of her son whom she adores and who adores her and engaging new acquaintances in the details of their mutual existence. Instead she has chosen to hold on to her position as the wife of a man well regarded in the community but who does not now, did not then and never will be in love with her. Position is evidently enough. Legitimacy is enough. The esteem in which she is held by her Circle of Frendz is enough. All of those are the things by which she has defined herself. So even if her looks fade, she can hold on to those other tangibles of her existence.

Perhaps it is by virtue of her mother, the out-of-wedlock, pregnant civil servant who had no prestige, virtually no standing in the limited environs of her community and who for some reason chose to hold herself and her illegitimate daughter in regard above most others by dint of some magical thinking, that Mrs. has allowed herself to accept a life that is so much less of what it could be in terms of the happiness quotient that could have been generated either by her or on her behalf. But after all, she is not a Baby Boomer demanding only the best—as does her son, a Boomer himself, who expects only the best.

And Mr., he of the fine mind and the still appealing appearance even into his mid-seventies, is amazingly willing to accept the mind-numbing, soul destroying life that she continues to provide. His journey with her into oblivion, whether at My Happy Retreat or abroad, will not be one based in fantasy and illusion, but rather in the clear and certain knowledge of what his life could have been like, but won't be like and will be like with her directing the ship of state. I can't even pretend to offer platitudes about his being of a generation that accepted the call of duty and self-sacrifice at all costs because there is enough of that to go around across the generations for all of us. The current specter of his life to come is what he, with full knowledge, has chosen for himself.

Maybe, in the end, he is in fact the loyal and faithful civil servant on one last deployment on behalf of Her Majesty the Queen because in some very real sense he is still serving at the pleasure of The Queen. Twenty-five years ago he chose to opt out, to vacate his position, to leave the British Foreign and Commonwealth Office and try his luck with an endeavor that he imagined would be under the complete control of his own hand. He would orchestrate his own happy retreat and pursue the life of a gentleman farmer, a country squire. But his life hasn't quite been as he imagined it would be.

He has made three attempts over the course of his marriage to escape from an anesthetizing domestic servitude, each escape lasting a few months longer than the last. His future, however, unlike hers, will not see him embracing a life of illusion but one of bitter truth. God help him though because he can't pretend not to know what awaits him in the years ahead compared to what might have been. More Sudoku, more crosswords, more dinners and buffet lunches where

> *In the room the women come and go*
> *Talking of Michelangelo.*

Hardly. In reality, nothing so high-minded of course. More likely endless prattle about the heat and how much more rain is needed.

> *S`io credesse che mia risposta fosse*
> *A persona che mai tornasse al mondo,*
> *Questa fiamma staria senza piu scosse.*
> *Ma perciocchè giammai di questo fondo*
> *Non tornò vivo alcun, s'i'odo il vero,*
> *Senza tema d'infamia ti rispondo.*

TONI M. FORSYTH

Translation:

If I but thought that my response were made
to one perhaps returning to the world,
this tongue of flame would cease to flicker.
But since, up from these depths, no one has yet
returned alive, if what I hear is true,
I answer without fear of being shamed.

"THE LOVE SONG OF J. ALFRED PRUFROCK"
—T.S. ELIOT

Perhaps they will both slowly retreat in silence into some inner world, each to his or her own, forever enshrined in the vision of the closed and bolted doors of My Happy Retreat.

About the Author

Toni Forsyth is Professor Emerita in English from a San Francisco, California South Bay two-year college. She is the author of several monographs on issues of governance and diversity in American higher education.

She was the Executive Producer, scriptwriter and moderator of a five-part teleconference series, "Multicultural Perspectives in Higher Education". She has also produced five national conferences on Diversity in Teaching and Learning in American Higher Education.

In 1987 with grant funding from the Ford Foundation, Dr. Forsyth founded Middle College High School at Los Angeles Southwest College. She lives in the Caribbean with her dogs Rusty and Moyu.

Acknowledgements

Many people over the years, both friends and family, have inspired my desire to branch out from academic writing into the world of fiction. My mother, to whom I have dedicated this novel, is first and foremost among them. I can clearly remember writing my first "book" at age seven or eight, on her pink stationery, while lying in bed next to her one evening. I know she preserved it for posterity, between the pages of my baby book where it still sits, merely awaiting discovery by some enterprising publisher.

But for more recent support and encouragement, I must thank my dear friends Donna Asimont and Ulysses Pichon for reading the manuscript in its entirety and providing the positive feedback necessary for me to follow through with its publication. For the latter, an academic colleague, it was never a matter of "If" but "When." His canny perspectives on life and the written word were the touchstone for many of my creative endeavours during my years in academia. The former, a medical doctor, provided confirmation about the psychological toll that the aging process can take; particularly among women who are taught from an early age that their youth and beauty above all else are their most desirable and marketable assets.

And I cannot conclude without thanking two additional people—my publisher, Lena Rose of Minna Press—and finally, my warmest and most heartfelt thanks to my dearest friend and inspiration to whom I read chapters on end aloud and who saw in me the person whose passion it was to write from the heart about the heart.